ALPHA MOON

RED MOON SERIES, BOOK FOUR

ELIZABETH KELLY

EK PUBLISHING INC.

ALPHA MOON

BOOK FOUR, RED MOON SERIES

Why does something so wrong feel so right?

Although human, Dani has lived her entire life among the Lycans. She knows first-hand their possessiveness toward their mates, and she's determined to avoid being claimed by one. It's one of the reasons she's in love with the human, Kaden, despite his love for her cousin.

When Andric, a Lycan without a pack, saves her life she's confused by her feelings. He's possessive, demanding and naughty – everything she swore she'd stay away from. So why does his touch spark desire in her belly? Why does she forget about her love for Kaden when she is in her arms?

CHAPTER 1

Dani sighed and stared morosely out the window of the common room. Her father, uncle and cousins had left yesterday to rescue Sophia and Kaden, and the entire household was anxious and tense. Last night Leta had been whiny and moody and Avery, normally sweet and patient with her obstinate young child, had lost her temper and snapped at her.

The rest of the family had stared in surprise as Leta's mouth dropped open and she gaped at her mother. Large, fat teardrops welled up in her eyes and dripped down her cheeks as Avery, her face strained and pale, picked her up and carried her to the rocking chair. She had whispered an apology and then rocked the softly weeping Lycan to sleep. Leo had offered to carry her to bed but Avery had declined. She had sat staring into the fire, holding Leta tightly as she rocked, and when Dani had finally gone to bed, Avery still hadn't moved from her spot.

A soft hand touched her head and Dani smiled at her mother. "Hello, Mama." She returned her gaze to the window.

"You've been sitting here all morning, dearest." Maya

stroked Dani's fine, blonde hair. "Come to the kitchen with me. We'll have some tea and wait together."

Dani shook her head. "No, thank you."

"Your father will be fine." Maya rested her head against Dani's. "He and the others will be back soon."

"I know," Dani replied. "It's Doran I'm worried about. They should be back from town by now."

"They would have stayed overnight and left early this morning," Maya reminded her gently.

"Aye, and it's almost lunch. They should be back," Dani said.

"Jeffrey is with them. He'll keep them safe," Maya said but Dani could hear the worry in her voice.

"There was a Gogmagog in the woods. Andric said they travel in packs. What if there are more?"

Maya kissed the top of her head. "Are you sure it was a Gogmagog, Dani? You've never seen one before and they stay in the outskirts, you know that."

Dani shook her head. "It was, Mama. Even Andric said it was and he's seen them before."

"Has he?" Maya said thoughtfully.

"What?" Dani asked.

"Nothing, dearest," Maya replied.

Dani rolled her eyes. "It's obviously something. What is it? Do you not like Andric?"

"I don't even know him." Maya smiled at her. "I guess I just find it strange that his entire pack was killed by leeches, but he survived. Did he tell you how he lived?"

Dani shook her head. "I've barely spoken to him since we got back. He hardly spoke a word at supper last night."

"Aye, he does seem to be a quiet one," Maya answered.

"He saved my life, Mama," Dani said.

"Aye, and I will always be grateful to him for that." Maya

kissed her forehead and squeezed her shoulder. "Are you sure you won't have a hot cup of tea? I'm making Avery one as well."

"Where is Aunt Avery?" Dani asked.

"She's in her room, resting."

"Is she ill? Is it because she healed Andric yesterday?" Dani asked in alarm. "I'm perfectly healthy. I can lie down with her for a while."

She started towards the door and Maya caught her arm. "No, dearest. She is just worried about her husband and her children. Leave her be for now."

Dani nodded, and Maya kissed her forehead before leaving the room. She stared out the window again and could have cried with relief when, fifteen minutes later, the wagon carrying Doran, Evan, and Jeffrey drove past the house and stopped in front of the barn.

She ran outside, her heart thudding loudly in her chest, and chased after it. Doran jumped down and she launched herself at her twin. He hugged her and she squeezed his arm. "Are you all right?"

"Aye. Why wouldn't I be?" He gave her a strange look as Evan, his face pale, climbed into the back of the wagon. Dani started forward and Doran pulled her back.

"No, Dani. Do not look."

"Doran -"

"No," he told her. "Go back to the house."

"Your brother is right." Jeffrey was unhitching the horses. "Go on, girl."

He led the horses into the barn as Evan said, "Doran, can you help me with him?"

"Aye." Doran gave Dani a gentle push. "Go tell Mama that we're back."

"I saw it happen!" Dani shouted. "I watched them take his

3

head! I watched him die and now you think you have to shelter me from his body? I am not a child, Doran! I want to see him. I want to say goodbye."

She lunged for the wagon and Doran caught her by the arm. She turned on him, kicking and flailing wildly, and Doran stared at her in shock.

He took her wrists and held them firmly, wincing when she kicked him in the shin. "Dani! What's wrong with you? Stop it, right now," he said.

"Shut up, Doran! You have no right to tell me what to do!" She screamed again.

She was twisting and squirming like a wildcat, and he flinched when she caught him again in the shin with her foot. She twisted free of his grasp and bolted for the wagon as he reached for her. His fingers skated across the back of her shirt and he cursed loudly.

"Dani, you don't want to see him. Trust me, please!" he pleaded as he chased after her.

She ignored him completely and scrambled toward the back of the wagon. She was only a few feet away when Andric appeared and stepped in front of her. She ran straight into him and bounced backward. He caught her neatly around the waist before she fell and she stared at him, her chest heaving and her eyes dark with panic.

"Listen to your twin, Danielle," he said.

She hesitated and then swung wildly at him. He caught her fist before it could connect with his jaw, brought it to his mouth and kissed her knuckles. "You should not see him like this."

"You can't tell me what to do!" she shouted and tried to yank her hand free before pounding on his back with her other one. She was beginning to cry, and he pulled her into his embrace.

4

"Shh, Danielle." He didn't seem to feel the blows she rained on his back, or the kicks she aimed at his legs.

"Dani?" Doran was standing beside them and she glared furiously at him.

"Leave me alone, Doran!"

Doran looked helplessly at Andric. The Lycan shrugged and then suddenly bent and simply heaved Dani over his shoulder.

"Let me go," she sobbed as he carried her away from the wagon and toward the smaller barn. "Let me go right now or you'll regret it!" She squirmed against him and then bit him hard on the back.

He grunted with pain but continued to the barn. He kicked the door shut and carried her into an empty stall before dropping her gently on her feet. He stepped back, blocking the doorway of the stall with his body, and gave her a look of sympathy.

"I am sorry, Danielle. I know you think you want to see him but, believe me, you do not."

She glared at him and then made a break for the side of the stall, gripping the edge of it and lifting herself nimbly toward the top. He cursed under his breath and grabbed her. Despite the fact that she was hanging on to the wood with all of her strength, he pulled her easily away from it.

She shrieked with anger and threw her weight backward. He staggered on his feet, tripped, and fell with a hard thump to the ground of the stall, dragging Dani down with him. Before she could scramble free, he had rolled and pinned her to the ground, throwing one hard leg over hers and pinning her arms above her head.

"Stop, Danielle," he said. "I am not letting you go."

She struggled wildly for a few more seconds and then as quickly as her anger had come upon her, it left. She slumped against the ground and stared up at him as tears slid down her cheeks. He released her arms cautiously and she immediately threw them around him and clutched tightly. She buried her face in his neck and sobbed as he stroked her waist and hip.

CHAPTER 2

"I'm sorry." Dani's voice was muffled against his throat.

"For what?" Andric continued to rub her side and hip.

"For hitting you, for crying and making a fool of myself," Dani replied. "I'm not usually such a – a crybaby."

He leaned back and smiled at her, wiping away the last of her tears from her cheeks. "I do not think you're a crybaby, Danielle."

She stared silently at him as his fingers lingered on her cheek. "You watched a friend die, you nearly died yourself, and your family is in grave danger. All things considered, you're doing remarkably well."

"Why did you offer to stay and protect us?" she whispered.

He shrugged. "No resistance for damsels in distress. Remember?"

"Aye, I remember," she murmured. A funny little tingle went through her stomach when Andric's gaze dropped to her mouth.

"Especially for one as pretty as you," he said.

Heat spread through her belly, sweet and not entirely

unwelcome, as he traced the line of her jaw with his callused fingers. Her pulse was quickening, and she could feel the heat in her belly spreading throughout her body. It made her limbs tingle and her cheeks flush, and he inhaled deeply before smiling.

"How old are you, Danielle? Are you even out of your teens, yet?"

"I am over twenty," she said a bit indignantly.

His grin widened. "Good."

His hand squeezed her hip before caressing the side of her thigh through her linen skirt. She swallowed nervously and stared at his mouth. He had nice lips, she decided. An image of kissing those lips flipped through her head. It brought on another flash of heat and without realizing it, her hips arched against him as a surge of liquid dampened her panties. He inhaled sharply and his hand tightened on her firm thigh. She gasped, and her hands clutched at his biceps. He stared at her mouth again.

"You're very sweet, Danielle. Did you know that?" he whispered. "You're so lovely and innocent."

"I – I'm not innocent," she stammered.

"Are you not?" His hand went back to its lazy stroking of her thigh. "Tell me, Danielle. Have you even kissed a man before?"

"I – yes." Technically she had kissed a man. She had kissed Kaden the night of his birthday. Of course, he had pushed her away before she could properly kiss him but still, it was mostly a kiss.

He was watching her face carefully and he arched his eyebrow at her. "Have you?"

"Yes!" she replied hotly. "Do you believe me to be a liar?"

8

He shook his head. "No, but there's something you're not telling me."

She pressed her lips together and stared up at the ceiling of the barn. Truthfully, Kaden pushing her away had been the most humiliating moment of her life. She knew it was because he was in love with Sophia, but there was still a small part of her that wondered if it was because of her. She wasn't as pretty as her Lycan cousin, but she wasn't ugly either. Her eyes were a lovely shade of blue, her skin smooth, and her blonde hair soft. Most Lycans didn't look twice at her though. They typically preferred their women to be curvier with tanned skin and dark hair.

"What are you hiding, Danielle?"

"Nothing," she lied.

"Did you enjoy kissing him?" he asked.

"It was very brief," she admitted.

"Why?" His hand moved from her thigh to her ribs and stroked her just below her breasts.

"He pushed me away."

"He's a fool."

"He isn't!" She defended Kaden immediately. "He's wonderful."

"Is he? Why did he push you away?" The tips of his fingers brushed the underside of her breast almost absent-mindedly, and a moan slipped out before she could stop it.

"Perhaps I am not very good at kissing," she muttered.

"Let's find out, shall we?" He captured her mouth with his before she had fully comprehended what he'd said.

She stiffened under him as he kissed her. His lips pulled at her bottom one, sucking it into his mouth and licking at it with his tongue and she moaned. She squeezed his arms and returned his kiss, opening her mouth eagerly so that he could slip his tongue inside.

He made a groan of approval and pressed her into the soft hay that covered the ground of the stall. His hands threaded through her hair and he held her head steady as he kissed and licked at her mouth. When he finally released her mouth, she gave a soft mew of disappointment and tried to kiss him again.

He shook his head and held hers firmly, preventing her from pressing her mouth against his. "He's a fool, Danielle."

"He's not," she whispered.

He ignored her and kissed the tip of her nose. "Do you have any idea of the things I want to do to you?"

She shivered at the raw need in his voice. "Aye. I told you, I am not innocent."

He grinned. "You are. In fact, it may be wise of you to stay away from me."

Despite his words, he made no effort to pull away from her. Instead, he settled himself more firmly against her and she swallowed nervously when she felt his erection against her hip.

"Why?"

"I have certain tastes that I fear you are too sweet for. I like the women who warm my bed to do things that you, unfortunately, will most likely not enjoy."

"What kind of things?" she whispered.

He shook his head. "Now is not the time to share. In fact, as pleasant as this is, I think it's time we stopped. I imagine your twin will be here any moment to check on you."

She tried to hide her disappointment and knew she'd failed when Andric grinned at her. "You want more of my kisses?"

She nodded immediately and without shame. "Aye, I do."

"Perhaps just one more," he whispered. He took her mouth again and Dani moaned and pressed herself against him. He took his time kissing her, exploring her mouth leisurely until she was squirming against him. When he cupped one breast through her shirt, she cried out into his mouth and gripped his arms.

He smiled against her mouth. "We really must stop now, Danielle. You have no idea what your innocent kisses do to me."

"Andric," she moaned as his thumb smoothed over her aching nipple.

"Of course, I'll be angry with myself later if I don't at least look at your breasts. You turned away so quickly in the forest I hardly had the chance to admire them." Without asking, he pushed her shirt up around her neck.

"They're so lovely," he whispered. He stared at them for so long that Danielle could feel embarrassment seeping past her desire. She had no idea what was so lovely about them. They were small and unremarkable.

When he continued to look at them without touching her, she tried to shove her shirt down. He shook his head and captured both of her wrists in one hand. He pinned her arms above her head and pushed her shirt up a bit more.

"Arch your back, Danielle," he suddenly demanded.

She stared at him in confusion. "Why?"

He gave her a stern look. "Do as I tell you."

"Not until you tell me why."

He sighed, and then his hand was on her hip and he had twisted her to her side and delivered a hard spank to her ass. She squealed in shock and pain as he flipped her back. She glared at him and twisted in his grip.

"Let go of me, you ass!" she snapped. "How dare you? I am not a child that you can just – just spank whenever you feel like it. Let go of me right now before I – ohhh…"

Her anger turned quickly to lust when his hot mouth

closed around one stiff nipple. He sucked firmly, teasing her nipple with the tip of his tongue, until she was panting and moaning beneath him. He released her nipple and smiled at her.

"Arch your back," he repeated.

She did as he asked, arching her back until her small breasts were nearly touching his mouth.

"So pretty," he murmured.

He captured her other nipple in his mouth and teased it to a stiff, aching point. Danielle pulled at the hand holding her wrists and he tightened his fingers around her delicate flesh.

"No," he whispered. "Stay just like this." He leaned down and kissed her again, sliding his tongue into her mouth while his other hand cupped and kneaded her small breasts.

"I love how responsive you are," he breathed against her mouth. "I bet you're soaking wet. Are you, Danielle? Is your pussy wet for me?"

She gave him a look of shock. "Andric, you – you shouldn't say such things to me."

He grinned at her. "Why not?"

"Because it's coarse," she whispered.

"Have I offended you?" He kissed her throat, licking and nipping at her skin, and she moaned again.

"Have I? Answer me or I'll spank you again," he said.

"You would not dare!" She glared at him.

"I would," he replied immediately. "Now tell me – have I offended you?"

She stared silently at him as she weighed her options. Her ass was still stinging from his earlier spank and she couldn't figure out why she was hesitating to answer him. She didn't like being spanked by Andric. Did she?

Before she could answer her own question, Andric winked at her and then quickly flipped her to her side and spanked her twice more. She yelled her outrage and he laughed. "I warned you, Danielle."

"Stop spanking me!" she snapped.

He stared at her small breasts. Her nipples were still hard, and he leaned down and licked her right one. She cried out with pleasure as he rubbed his rough stubble in the hollow of her breasts. He released her wrists and reached under her to gently rub her burning ass.

She moaned again and he pressed his shirt-covered chest against her naked one. She stared into his eyes as her arms crept around his shoulders. He studied her carefully for a few moments before sighing. "You are too sweet and innocent for someone like me."

She scowled at him. "Why does everyone call me sweet? I'm not sweet or innocent."

He laughed. "Are you not then?"

"No!" Determined to prove it to him, she reached down and grabbed his firm ass. She squeezed it and pushed her pelvis against him.

He laughed delightedly and kissed her again. "My, you are a bold little thing, aren't you? Of course, I shouldn't be surprised. You did try and take on a Gogmagog, after all."

She flushed with pleasure when he gave her an admiring look. "You were very brave in the forest, Danielle."

"Thank you," she whispered.

"But that does not mean you're not sweet and innocent," he teased.

She gave him her own slap to the ass, and he jerked against her and cursed under his breath. "Behave yourself, Danielle."

"And if I don't?" she asked, feeling a strange, sweet madness coursing through her veins. "Will you spank me again?"

"Aye," he answered. "Only this time, I'll put you over my knee, lift your skirt, and spank you properly."

Another flash of heat swept through her belly and she squeezed her thighs together. The thought of being sprawled over Andric's lap while he spanked her with his hard hand, was doing things to her insides that both confused and excited her. She was embarrassed to realize that her panties were soaking wet, and her cheeks reddened as Andric grinned down at her.

"I think you like that idea, innocent Danielle."

"No, I don't," she denied. "I'm not a child."

"Aye, I am well aware of that." He gazed at her naked breasts again. "There's nothing wrong with liking it."

She took a deep breath. "Do other women enjoy it?"

"Aye, some do," he replied.

"Truly?"

He kissed her lightly. "Truly. And I am both pleasantly surprised and delighted that you enjoy it."

"I – I don't," she protested.

"No?" He grinned at her. "So, if I were to put my hand between your thighs right now, I would not find your pussy wet?"

A shudder of desire went through her. "Andric, you should not speak to me that way."

"Aye, so you keep saying." He gripped her thigh in his hand and tugged. "Open your legs, Danielle."

"Andric…"

"Open them," he coaxed before kissing her again. She returned his kiss as her thighs loosened and he slid his hand under her skirt. His fingers traced her inner thigh and he pushed until her legs were spread as far as her skirt would allow.

"Good girl," he whispered against her mouth, and another

shiver of need went through her.

He kissed her throat again, licking and sucking as his fingers traced tiny circles on the sensitive skin of her thigh. Dani stared up at the ceiling of the barn. She couldn't seem to catch her breath, and small moans and sighs were escaping from between her lips. Andric was still tracing circles on her thigh and she wanted to grab his hand and shove it upward. Her pussy was throbbing in a way she had never felt before, and her entire body felt like it was on fire.

"Andric, please," she moaned.

"Patience, Danielle," he whispered into her ear.

"Please, I can't -"

"Danielle?"

Her mother's voice had her jerking away from Andric. She shoved her shirt down as he relaxed on his side and propped up his head with his hand. He grinned as she stumbled to her feet.

"Hello, Mama."

"Are you okay, dearest? Doran said you were upset, and that Andric brought you in here." Maya looked around curiously. "Where is Andric?"

"He – he left." Dani leaned against the stall wall. She rested her arms across the top of it and gave her mother a nervous smile.

"Do you want to talk about it?" Maya started down the wide aisle of the barn as Danielle felt Andric squirm between her legs and sit between them. He rested his back against the stall, and she risked a quick look down. He was grinning up at her and she clamped her thighs together as he slid his hands up her skirt.

Maya stopped to pet Bella. The horse nudged her arm and Maya rubbed her broad nose gently.

"No, Mama. I'm fine. I – I just want to be alone, please."

Andric's hands were rubbing the front of her thighs and they trembled in response. He pulled firmly on her thighs as he leaned forward and placed a kiss through her skirt on her throbbing, hot core.

She gasped and her hands squeezed the top of the stall compulsively as Maya frowned at her. "Dani, I know what happened to Ian was upsetting, and I know you're worried about your father and," she paused, "Kaden. You can't keep it bottled inside, my love. You'll feel better if you talk about what happened."

Dani barely heard her mother. Andric had pried her thighs apart and his hand was slowly inching up her soft skin. He buried his face into her crotch and inhaled deeply as his hand quickly cupped her pussy possessively. Only the wet material of her panties separated her needy flesh from his warm hand, and she could feel her face reddening as his other hand slipped around her to cup her ass. He squeezed her ass and she kicked his leg with her foot. He grunted and his hand tightened on her pussy.

"Dani? Are you listening to me?" Maya frowned at her.

"Aye, Mama," Dani said. She pulled away from Andric and hurried out of the stall without looking at him. "You're right. I shouldn't keep it bottled up inside. Will you come to the kitchen with me and have a cup of tea?"

"Of course." Maya put her arm around Dani. "Are you feeling all right, Dani?"

"Aye, why?"

"You're flushed." Maya put her hand on Dani's forehead.

"I'm fine." Dani smoothed her skirt and smiled at her mother. "Let's go, Mama."

At the door to the barn, she took a quick look over her shoulder. Andric popped his head over the stall and winked at her. She blushed and hurried after her mother.

CHAPTER 3

"Doran, what have you done?" Maya hurried into the kitchen. Doran was standing at the sink, rinsing the blood from his hand.

"It's nothing, Mama. I just cut my hand a little."

She took his hand and frowned at the wide, deep cut across the palm of his hand. "How did this happen?"

"I was helping to dig Ian's grave. The ground is partially frozen, and the shovel broke in my hands. I sliced it on the broken handle, I think."

"Oh, Doran." She pressed a dish towel to his hand and brushed his hair back from his face.

"It's fine. It'll be healed in a few hours." Doran smiled at her.

"I could ask Avery to -"

Doran shook his head. "No, do not. Aunt Avery has enough to worry about."

Maya frowned. "She wouldn't mind, Doran. Avery would not -"

She broke off as a pale and silent Avery entered the kitchen.

"How are you, honey?" Maya asked.

"Fine," Avery said. "Worried, but fine."

"Aye, I know." Maya squeezed her arm as Avery stood in front of Doran. She frowned at the blood-soaked towel wrapped around his hand.

"Let me see your hand, my love."

"It's fine, Aunt Avery," Doran said.

Without speaking, Avery unwrapped the towel from around his hand and studied the wound carefully before pressing the towel around it again. She pulled Doran into her embrace and held him closely.

"Aunt Avery, you don't have to do this," he protested.

"Hush, Doran." She hugged him tightly and he returned her hug as Maya started the tea.

———

"THANK YOU, AUNT AVERY." DORAN FLEXED HIS HAND AND then lifted the mug to his mouth. He took a drink of the hot tea as Avery smiled at him.

"You're welcome, my love. How did you hurt your hand?"

"The shovel broke while I was helping to," he hesitated, "dig Ian's grave."

Avery sighed and squeezed Maya's hand. "Poor Ian. I can't believe he's gone."

Tears were starting to drip down her cheeks, and Maya sniffed and wiped at the moisture on her own cheeks. "I'm so sorry, Avery. I know how fond you were of him."

Jeffrey entered the kitchen, his cheeks and nose red from the cold, and stared at them soberly. "How is your hand, Doran?"

"Aunt Avery healed it for me," Doran replied. "Are you finished already?"

Jeffrey sighed and gave Avery a quick look. "I've brought the young Evan back. He was fine while we were digging the grave and he insisted on helping us put Ian's body in the ground. I'm afraid it was upsetting to him when we started to fill the grave."

"Where is he?" Avery asked.

"He's in the smaller barn, my lady. He's – he's crying, and he didn't want to worry you," Jeffrey said.

"Thank you, Jeffrey." She stood and then hugged the stout Lycan. "Are you all right?"

"Aye, my lady." Jeffrey gave her a shaky smile.

"Sit and have some tea and warm up." She squeezed his arm and guided him to the table.

He sat down with a weary sigh as Doran stood up. "I'll go and finish filling Ian's grave."

Jeffrey shook his head. "Andric is doing it. He showed up just after you left and helped us finish digging the grave. When Evan started getting so upset, he told me to take him back to his mother, he would finish up."

As Avery left the kitchen, Maya poured Jeffrey a cup of tea. He nodded gratefully and sipped at it as Doran drummed his fingers on the table.

"Where is Dani?" he asked suddenly.

"She's resting in her room," Maya replied.

"Did she talk to you?" he asked.

"Aye. We spoke a little about what happened in town."

"She was so upset, Mama. I have never seen her that way before," Doran said.

"She'll be fine, dearest." Maya smiled at him.

"I'm going to go check on her." Doran stood and left the room as Maya sipped at her tea.

Jeffrey touched her hand. "Your husband and the others will be fine, my lady. They will return soon with Sophia and Kaden."

"Aye, I know," she replied with a confidence she didn't feel.

Renee entered the kitchen and Jeffrey watched her closely as she washed her hands at the sink. "Hello, Maya. Hello, Jeffrey."

"Hello, Renee."

Maya watched with amusement as Jeffrey's ruddy face turned even redder.

"How are you today?" he asked.

Renee shrugged. "I'll feel better when everyone returns home safely." She squeezed Maya's shoulder and headed down the hallway to her room. Jeffrey watched her go, and then blushed again when he glanced at Maya.

"You should just ask her out, Jeffrey."

He scoffed a bit. "Ask her out? I am not a teenage Lycan, my lady. I am well past the age of asking a woman out."

She smiled. "You know what I mean."

He stared down at the table. "Renee and I have known each other for over two decades, Maya."

"Aye, and I have watched you pine for her for at least a decade of that."

"If she were interested in me, she would have made it known by now," he replied. "Besides, she is dating that human from the Billings household – Kristoff."

Maya shook her head. "No, she is not. Did you not hear? They parted ways."

Jeffrey glanced up at her in shock. "What? When?"

"At least two moons ago. It was around the time that we brought Vivian back."

"I did not know that," Jeffrey replied.

"Aye. I guess Kristoff wanted her to move to the city with him. She didn't want to leave the country, she said."

Maya smiled. "I remember when we were bought from the slave house by Tristan. Renee was most upset that we were going to be living in the country."

Jeffrey grunted in reply and Maya gave him an earnest look. "You must at least try, Jeffrey. The worst that can happen is she says no."

"Now you sound like Ian."

Maya smiled again. "He did seem to become a bit of a matchmaker in his later years, did he not?"

"Aye. Yet, he did not find another after his mate died. I do not know why. He was lonely. I know he was. I never met his Anna, but I don't believe she would have wanted him to spend the rest of his life alone. Do you?"

Maya wiped at the tears that were starting to slide down her cheeks. "He is with his Anna now."

"Aye, he is." Jeffrey stared down at the table as Leta wandered into the kitchen.

"Hello, Leta." Maya smiled at the girl.

"Hi," Leta said quietly. She stood beside Jeffrey and held her arms out. He pushed his chair back and lifted her into his lap. She curled into him and rested her head on his wide chest. "Where's Mama?"

"She's in the barn with Evan." Jeffrey patted her back and she took his other hand and traced the dark hairs on the back of it.

"I want Papa to come home."

"I know." Jeffrey kissed the top of her head. "He will be home soon."

"I should have gone with him," Leta said.

"You are too little, Leta," Jeffrey replied.

"I am not!" She sat up and glared at him, her eyes glowing green. "I am big enough to fight!"

Jeffrey smiled at her and squeezed her chin. "I have no doubt that you are as tough as Lycan claws, but you must grow a bit more."

She sighed and leaned against his chest, staring across the table at Maya. "Will they be back soon?"

"Aye," Maya said. "They will, dearest."

Leta sighed again, and Jeffrey shifted her on his lap. "Leta, why don't you come with Leo and me to the west field? We need to mend the fence and could use your help."

"All right." Leta slid off his lap and took Jeffrey's hand as he stood. They left the kitchen, and Maya stood and stared out the window over the sink. She sipped at her tea, sending a silent prayer to the gods that they would bring Marshall home safe to her.

———

ANDRIC HAD JUST FINISHED PILING THE LAST OF THE ROCKS on the grave when the old Lycan appeared. She walked slowly, holding her jacket around her, and he stepped back when she stood beside the grave.

"It needs a cross." Her voice was low.

"Aye. I will make one."

She stared steadily at him. "Why would you do that? You did not even know Ian."

"True," he acknowledged.

They were quiet for a few minutes and then he said, "Did you know him well?"

"Aye. Ian's father and my husband were good friends. Ian was quite a bit older than our boy, but he was always kind to him. Tristan was forever trailing after Ian and his friends."

She smiled. "He was so patient with Tristan. Years ago, when Ian's wife died, Tristan asked him to come live with him and work in the barns. Ian accepted and he became a part of our family. He was a good man."

He could see tears starting to fall and he cleared his throat. "I'm sorry for your loss, my lady."

"I have forgotten your name," she said briskly as she wiped at her cheeks.

"Andric." He held his hand out and she shook it.

"Vivian Williams."

"It's nice to meet you, Mrs. Williams."

"Aye, you as well. I never thanked you for saving my granddaughter."

"I'm glad I could help her."

"Awfully convenient that you were there, wasn't it?" she said.

He shrugged. "Lucky, is more like it."

"Why did you help Dani? Why would you risk your life for a human you don't even know?" she asked.

He blew his breath out and stared at the ground. "I have seen enough death the last few moons. I had no wish to see an innocent girl lose her life as well."

"Your entire pack was killed by leeches, am I remembering correctly?"

"Aye."

She waited for him to elaborate and when he didn't, she sighed impatiently. "Are you always this quiet, Andric."

"Aye, my lady."

"Because you have something to hide?"

He shook his head. "No, my lady."

She regarded him carefully for a few moments. "Where are you from?"

"My pack lived about forty miles outside of the town called Morden. Do you know it?"

"Aye. I have heard of it. It's to the north, close to the outskirts. Full of thieves and murderers, I've heard."

He nodded. "That it is."

"Why did your pack live so close to the outskirts?"

He hesitated. "My pack leader had an issue with humans. He did not care for them and wished to be as far from them as possible. There are not many humans that live near the outskirts."

"Why did he dislike the humans?"

"I do not know."

"Do you have a problem with humans?" she asked.

He shook his head. "No, my lady. Not all of the pack members shared our leader's view of the humans. My mother taught me as a pup to respect both Lycans and humans."

"When my sons return, will you continue on to Vanden?"

"Aye."

She stared down at Ian's grave for a moment before turning away. Andric held his arm out to the old Lycan. "May I walk you back to the house, Mrs. Williams?"

She took his arm. "Aye, you may."

CHAPTER 4

"Vivian! What happened?" Avery and Bree hurried out from the house. Vivian was being carried by Andric and she gave Avery a look of embarrassment.

"I'm fine, Avery. Just tripped and twisted my ankle a bit." She glanced up at Andric. "It would have been much worse if this one hadn't been there to keep me mostly on my feet."

He smiled and shifted her in his arms as Avery put her hand on Vivian's arm. "Could you carry her to her room?"

"Aye, my lady," Andric said.

"Just carry me into the house. I can walk from there," Vivian replied. "You've been carrying me for nearly ten minutes and I'm heavy. Your arms must be ready to fall off."

Andric grinned as he carried her into the house. "Nonsense, my lady. You are as light as a feather."

Vivian scoffed. "Flattery will get you nowhere, Andric. Put me down, I can walk to my bedroom."

"It has been a long time since I've carried a beautiful woman to her bedroom. Surely you would not be so cruel as to deny me that pleasure now?" Andric replied.

Bree and Avery watched as Vivian flushed deeply and a

small grin crossed her face. "I believe I said that flattery would get you nowhere, young man."

"Indeed you did, my lady. But I fear I cannot help myself when faced with beauty such as yours." Andric winked at her and Avery stumbled to a stop behind them when Vivian giggled.

Andric carried her down the hallway. "Now which way to your bedroom, my lady?"

Avery looked down at Bree in astonishment. "Did you – did Vivian just giggle?"

Bree laughed. "Aye, Mama. I believe she did."

"The gods be damned," Avery muttered. She hurried down the hallway to Vivian's bedroom as Bree trailed after her.

Andric was just placing Vivian on the bed and Avery and Bree watched as he lifted Vivian's hand to his mouth. He placed a soft kiss on her knuckles. "A few days rest and you'll be ready to dance."

Vivian giggled again and Andric smiled at her before nodding to Avery and Bree and leaving the room. Vivian smoothed down her skirt as the two women stared silently at her.

"What?" she said a bit crossly, her cheeks reddening.

"Nothing." Avery cleared her throat and sat down on the bed beside Vivian. She placed her hands on the old woman's ankle and smiled at her.

"He's a nice boy," Vivian said defensively.

"He does seem very charming." Avery grinned as Bree snickered behind her.

Vivian flushed again. "That's enough giggling from the two of you. Do you hear me?"

"Aye, my lady," Avery said sweetly. "You seem to be doing enough giggling for all of us."

Bree laughed again and Vivian gave her an affectionate look, tinged with exasperation. She flapped her hand at her as she settled back against the pillows. "Go on with you now."

Bree grinned at her. "I'll just go and get you some tea while Mama heals you, all right?"

"Aye, thank you," Vivian replied.

———

DANI STARED GLUMLY OUT THE COMMON ROOM WINDOW. Behind her, she could hear her grandmother laughing at something Andric said to her. It was late afternoon and Andric had neither looked at nor spoken to her since she had come down from her bedroom. She crossed her arms and sighed.

She had temporarily lost her mind that was all. Her worry for her father and the others, her sorrow over Ian's death, had made her vulnerable to Andric's warm touch. She was in love with Kaden and it was his touch she craved, not Andric's. It was unfortunate that Kaden loved her cousin, but that was no reason for her to just fall into the arms of another man. Besides, as far as she knew, neither Kaden nor Sophia had confessed their love to each other. She might still have a chance with Kaden.

Stop being such a foolish little girl. Kaden loves Sophia and he will never love you.

She tamped down the vicious little voice in her head and rubbed at her forehead wearily. What type of person did it make her, she wondered, to be in love with one man yet be willing to let another touch her so intimately? She thought back to the way Andric had kissed her, at how it felt when his mouth sucked at her nipple, and she shivered. It would not do to think about that. She had made a mistake - one she would not make again.

And when Kaden comes back and is still as in love with your cousin as ever? Will you finally see your foolishness for what it is and stop pining for him?

She rubbed her forehead again before staring out the window at the forest beyond the yard. She was being –

She gasped and stared wide-eyed out the window.

"Dad!" she shouted. Ignoring the other's startled looks, she fled out of the house. She ran across the yard and launched herself at her father. He caught her and hugged her tightly as she rained kisses down on his face.

"Daddy! Are you okay? Where are the others?" she asked worriedly as the others came hurrying up to them.

"I'm fine, Dani." He smiled at her reassuringly and set her down. Maya threw herself into his arms.

"Marshall! Oh, honey." She kissed him hard on the mouth and he returned her kiss before smiling at her.

"Hello, gorgeous. Don't cry." He wiped at the tears on her face before turning to the others.

Avery, her face pale and her mouth trembling, gave him a look of fear. "Marshall -"

"They're fine, my lady. Everyone is safe. We rescued Kaden and Sophia, and Draken and the others are dead."

Avery sank to her knees and buried her hands in her face. "Thank the gods."

"Where are they?" Vivian asked as Leta ran to her mother and wormed her way on to her lap.

"They went to rescue the humans that were left at Draken's home," Marshall said.

"They what?" Vivian nearly shouted.

"They could not leave them to suffer, mother. You know that," Marshall said.

"Are we going after them, Dad?" Doran asked.

Marshall shook his head. "No."

"Why not?" Doran frowned. "They may need our help."

"They won't. They'll help the other humans and be home soon. Do not worry," Marshall said.

"Marshall?" Avery said. "Are you sure that Sophia was not," she glanced down at Leta sitting in her lap, "hurt in any way?"

Marshall nodded. "Aye. She is perfectly fine, Avery. She was the one who took Draken's head."

Avery nodded with relief and Bree crouched down beside her. "Come, Mama. You should not be sitting on the cold ground."

She tugged Leta from Avery's lap and then helped her stand. Her small face was pinched with worry and Avery stroked her hair. "Do not worry, sweet Bree. James will come home to you."

"Aye, I know." Bree gave her a trembling smile. "Let's get inside. It is freezing out here."

MARSHALL TOOK A BITE OF VENISON AND STARED SHREWDLY at Andric across the dinner table. "Now that I have returned, I imagine you will be continuing on to Vanden tomorrow, will you not?"

Before Andric could reply, Danielle gave her father a dirty look. "Dad! You're being rude."

Marshall glanced at his daughter. "His protection is no longer required, Dani. It is rude of us to detain him any longer."

"It doesn't mean he has to leave right away!" she

protested hotly. Her father stared at her in a considering way and she blushed and stared down at her plate.

Marshall turned to Andric. "Thank you for your help, Andric. I appreciate everything you've done for my family."

"It was my pleasure," Andric replied.

"You know," Vivian set her wine glass down with a harsh thump, "personally, I would feel better if Andric stayed a few more days. Just until Tristan and the others return."

"You doubt my ability to protect you, Mother?" Marshall asked.

"Of course not. Don't be foolish, boy," Vivian said crossly. "But with everything that has happened, I believe it would be wise for us to take advantage of added help. As does Avery. Don't you, Avery?"

She peered at Avery, who stared blankly at her.

"Don't you, Avery," Vivian said pointedly.

"Aye, I do, Vivian," Avery replied with a quick glance at Dani.

"We cannot impose upon Andric any longer than we already have, Mother," Marshall protested.

"Nonsense! Andric doesn't mind. Do you, child?"

"Not at all, my lady." Andric grinned at her. "It would be an honour to stay with you and your family for a few more days."

"I suppose you feel the same way." Marshall glanced at Maya.

Dani, her fingers clenched tightly around her glass, stared at her mother. Maya smiled at her before patting Marshall's hand. "I do, my lord."

"Then it's settled," Vivian said briskly. "Andric will stay with us until Tristan and the others return. I believe it's a very wise decision."

"Aye, as does Dani, no doubt," Doran said.

"Shut up, Doran!" Dani glared at her twin as she blushed fiercely.

"I DO NOT LIKE THE WAY HE LOOKS AT HER."

"Who, my lord?" Maya asked as she slipped into her night dress.

Marshall gave her a wry look. "You know who I'm talking about. Do not pretend otherwise."

Maya grinned at him before unbuttoning his shirt. "Andric is a very nice young man."

"You would not be saying that if you were Lycan," Marshall protested. "His scent when he is around her speaks of his true intentions."

Maya pushed his shirt off his shoulders before tossing it into the basket on the floor. "Dani is a grown woman, my love. You cannot protect her forever."

"She is barely out of her teens!" Marshall unbuttoned his pants and shoved them down his legs.

"I was only twenty when I met you," Maya pointed out gently. Marshall followed her to the bed and climbed in beside her as she blew out the candle.

She rested her head on Marshall's chest and traced his chest hair as Marshall stared up at the ceiling. "That was different."

"How?"

"My intentions towards you were very honourable."

Maya laughed and sat up. "Were they now? I hate to tell you this, dearest, but my father would not have found your intentions honourable."

She grinned at him. "Do you not remember that night in

the pantry at Vivian's house? I don't believe what you did to me that night would be considered honourable."

Marshall blushed. "It is not my fault you were so lovely. I could hardly be expected to resist kisses that were as sweet as yours."

She giggled. "Wise answer, my lord."

"She hardly knows him. None of us do. He could be dangerous, for all we know."

"Your mother seems to like him, as do I. Do you doubt our judge of character?"

"No, but men like Andric – men who know how to be charming and polite – are the ones you need to be careful around," he said.

Maya rubbed his chest soothingly. "You would know, dear heart."

"What's that supposed to mean?" He raised his eyebrow at her, and she giggled again.

"You were the most charming man I ever met, Marshall. You charmed the pants off of me." She paused for a beat. "Literally."

He blushed again and she leaned down and kissed him on the mouth. "Dani is no longer a child and she likes Andric. There is nothing wrong with giving her the opportunity to get to know him better. There are not many options for her this far out in the country."

"She doesn't know who she likes. Two days ago, she was in love with Kaden!" Marshall said heatedly.

"She is young, my lord. She -"

"Aye, that is my point! She is young and she needs to be protected until she knows what she wants. She goes from wanting Kaden to wanting Andric within a matter of days. That's not a sign of her maturity."

Maya sighed. "Marshall, sometimes it is difficult at

Dani's age to know what you want."

"You knew."

"Aye, but I am not Dani. She is a smart girl, but I fear she has been a bit sheltered. You can't judge her for wanting to spread her wings with Andric."

He gave her an alarmed look. "Tell me she has not -" he shook his head. "No, I would smell it on the both of them."

He stared up at the ceiling as he tucked his arms behind his head. "If I smell him on her, I will -"

"You will do nothing, my lord," Maya said. "It is none of our business what Dani does with Andric."

"She is our daughter! Of course, it is our business!"

"She is not a child," Maya said. "I know you love her and want to protect her, but what she does with Andric is her business and her business alone. Do not embarrass her by treating her like a child in front of him."

Marshall sighed as Maya laid down and curled her body into his. "I do not want her to get hurt, Maya."

"I know, dear heart. I do not either, but I don't believe he will hurt her."

"You don't know that."

"Aye, I suppose I don't." She stared up at him. "Do not forget that he saved her life, my lord. Our child would be dead if not for him."

He sighed again. "I know."

"Will you do me a favour? Will you at least give Andric a chance?" Maya asked.

"Aye, Maya. I will," Marshall replied.

She smiled at him before taking his hand and leading it to her breast. "Good. Now, will you do me another favour? Will you show me how much you have missed me?"

He squeezed her breast and kissed her before whispering, "Aye, Maya. I will."

CHAPTER 5

"It is late. Why are you not tucked away in your warm bed?"

Dani's stomach twisted with nerves when she heard Andric's low voice behind her. She clasped her hands together and continued to stare out the window of the common room. "I couldn't sleep."

"Why not?" Andric was standing directly behind her now, and she shivered all over when his hand brushed away her curtain of blonde hair and he placed a soft kiss on the back of her neck.

"I – I am worried," she said as he slid his arm around her waist and rested his hand intimately against her flat stomach.

He placed another soft kiss on the side of her neck, this time tasting her with his tongue, and she moaned quietly.

"Worried for your family?"

"Aye." She stepped forward, wanting to distance herself from his warm touch, but he immediately pulled her back against him.

"Where are you going?"

"I – nowhere," she whispered.

"Perhaps I could help you sleep." His hand made wide circles on her stomach. "I know of several very pleasant techniques to help you."

She ignored her shiver of need and cleared her throat. "Will you tell me what happened to your pack, Andric? How you survived?"

He stiffened against her and this time it was she who drew him back to her. "Please, Andric."

"It is not a story for someone as sweet as you, Danielle," he said.

"I would hear it, anyway," she replied. She stroked his hand where it still rested against her stomach. "Please."

"No," he said. "A story like that will not help you sleep. Trust me." He kissed the side of her neck again before nuzzling his face into her hair. "Come, Danielle. I will tuck you into your warm bed. Perhaps you will allow me to show you an enjoyable way to tire out a person."

His hand drifted down to just above her pubic bone and rubbed lightly.

"Andric, I – I am in love with another," she blurted out.

His hand paused before beginning to circle her belly through her thin nightdress again. "Are you?"

"Aye, I am. I'm sorry," she whispered.

"Do not be. Being in love is never something to be sorry about." He sucked lightly on her earlobe and she groaned breathlessly.

"Who is the lucky man?" he murmured into her ear.

"His name is Kaden."

He paused and then cupped her face, turning it until she was looking at him. "Kaden? Is he not the human who belongs to your cousin?"

"I – how do you know that?"

He shrugged. "I have spoken with your twin and with Evan."

"He doesn't belong to her," Danielle said crossly. "You damn Lycans are so ridiculous with your, 'you belong to me' possessive bullshit."

He laughed softly. "So, it does not bother you that you have no Lycan genes?"

"No. I like being human like Mama. We're much more rational and calmer than Lycans," she said defiantly.

"Are you now?" He slid his hand up until the tips of his fingers brushed against the underside of her breast.

"Aye." She inhaled sharply and tugged at his hand. "Did you not hear me, Andric? I am in love with another."

"Aye, I heard you." He inhaled deeply. "But you want me."

"No, I don't," she muttered.

He laughed again, the sound reverberating through his chest and into her back. "Of course, you don't."

She flushed and he sucked on her neck. "Is this Kaden the one who pushed you away when you kissed him?"

At her hesitation, he slid his hand between their bodies and squeezed her ass. "Do not lie to me, Danielle. You know what will happen if you do."

A shudder of desire went through her at the thought of Andric spanking her right there in the common room.

He inhaled again and when he gripped her hip and pulled her back against him, she was not surprised to feel his erection pressing into her ass. "On second thought, go ahead and lie to me if that is what you want. I have no objections to spanking your lovely ass again."

"Aye, he is the one," she said hurriedly.

"Is he in love with your cousin?"

"I don't know," she lied.

He slid his hand under her night dress and slapped her bare ass. She jerked in his arms and glared at him. "Stop that!"

"I told you not to lie to me. Is he in love with her?"

"Aye," she said. "He is."

"Yet, you are still in love with him."

"You can't help who you fall in love with," she said.

"I suppose not." He suddenly cupped her breast. "Has he touched you like this?"

"You know he has not," she replied. "He is in love with my cousin."

"He is a fool," he whispered.

"Stop saying that!" She twisted her head and glared at him. "I told you before, he is wond-"

He kissed her hard on the mouth and she hesitated only briefly before kissing him back. He groaned his approval and turned her in his arms, pulling her up against him as he encouraged her to slide her tongue into his mouth. He sucked hard on it and she thrust her pelvis at him helplessly. His hands were slipping inside the neckline of her night dress and cupping her bare breasts before she realized what was happening.

He tugged on her nipples, rubbing and circling until they were hard pebbles, as he kissed her slowly and thoroughly. Dani moaned with pleasure before suddenly pulling her mouth from his.

"Andric!" she gasped. "We cannot do this."

"Why not?" He bent his head and licked the side of her neck.

"Because I – I am in love with another, and you said before that I was too sweet and innocent for you," she moaned.

"Aye, that is true." He gave her a look of regret before

stepping away from her. She swayed a little on her feet and he steadied her briefly before letting go. "I fear you have bewitched me, Danielle. I find it most difficult to resist your sweetness. But that is no excuse. I am sorry. Good night."

He turned and headed for the doorway and she took a few steps toward him. "Andric!"

"Aye?" He didn't turn around.

"I – nothing. Good night," she replied.

"Good night."

"Danielle?"

"Aye, Mama?"

"What is wrong, dearest?"

Danielle shook her head and smiled at her mother before returning her gaze to her bedroom window. "Nothing. I am fine."

Maya sat down on the bed beside her and looked out the window. Doran and Evan were fighting with swords as Andric watched with a look of amusement. He shook his head when Doran held out his sword to him.

Faintly through the window, Dani could hear her twin trying to coax Andric into taking the sword. "Come, you should try. We can teach you. Can't we, Evan?"

"Aye." Evan swung his sword in a wide arc. "I'm not as good as Nicky but I know enough."

Dani and Maya watched as Andric shook his head again. "No, I have no need for a sword. I am a Lycan."

"Aye, as are we. But it never hurts to learn different ways to protect yourself," Evan replied.

He sounded so much like Tristan that Maya couldn't suppress her grin. "He grows more and more like his father

39

every day. Vivian says that when Tristan was a boy he was as quiet as Evan. Although his love was for horses, not the arts like Evan's interest."

"Uncle Tristan is still quiet," Dani pointed out.

"Aye, that is true," Maya agreed.

"Do you think it bothers Uncle Tristan that Evan isn't a typical Lycan?" Dani asked.

Maya shook her head. "No. Tristan loves all of his children."

"I know that." Dani frowned. "But do you think it bothers him that Evan is more – more sensitive than most Lycans? The way that it bothers Daddy that I am not a Lycan."

Maya stared at her in surprise. "Danielle, your father does not care that you are not a Lycan."

"Does he not?" Dani asked.

"Of course not. He married a human and he is half-human himself. Why would you ever think that you being a human bothers him?"

"I don't know. He has been avoiding me ever since he returned from rescuing Sophia and Kaden. It's been three days, and I've barely seen him. I feel like in the last few years, we are not as close as we once were."

Maya hugged her. "It is because you are no longer his little girl, Danielle. He is torn between wanting to protect you and letting you live your own life. He finds it difficult to let go of his memories of you as his baby girl."

"Do you think so?"

"I know so," Maya said. "And now that Andric is here, and your father can smell how much you like him it is just one more sign that you are an adult. He will learn to deal with it, dearest. He just needs more time."

Dani gave her mother a cautious look. "I do not like Andric."

40

"Do you not?" Maya grinned at her. "Your father might argue that fact."

"Ugh." Dani made a face and stared down at the quilt. "Sometimes I hate living with Lycans. Do you know how embarrassing it is to have your own father and brother know that you – you want someone?"

"I'm sorry, Dani." Maya hugged her. "I know it is not always easy being a human in a family of Lycans." She hesitated. "Do you want to talk about Andric?"

Dani shook her head. She was close to her mother, but she had no desire to talk with her about her lust for the Lycan. "No, I do not. There is nothing to talk about. I am in love with Kaden."

Her mother's voice was soft with sympathy. "You know he is in love with Sophia."

"Aye, I know," Dani said grumpily. "Can I be alone, Mama? I'm tired."

"Of course." Maya slid off the bed and kissed Dani lightly on the forehead before leaving the room.

Dani sighed and flopped back on the bed. She stared at the ceiling and tried to block out both the memory of Andric's warm kisses and her shameful desire for more.

"RENEE, LET ME TAKE THOSE WATER BUCKETS. THEY ARE TOO heavy for you to be carrying." Jeffrey hurried down the hallway after Renee.

"It's fine, Jeffrey. I am stronger than I look," Renee said cheerfully.

"I insist, let me take them." He reached for the handles of the buckets and Renee gave him an odd look.

"It's fine. I carry these all the time. I don't need – oh!"

She gasped with surprise when Jeffrey pulled sharply on the buckets and they tipped in her hands. Hot water spilled down the front of her pants and into her shoes and Jeffrey turned bright red.

"I am so sorry, Renee!" He looked around frantically for something to sop the water up.

Renee gave a small hiss of pain and pulled her pants away from her legs. "Gods be damned! That burns!"

Jeffrey, his ruddy face paling, stared anxiously at her. "Are you hurt?"

Renee lifted one foot and then the other. "No, the water is just hot and I -"

She squealed in surprise when Jeffrey suddenly bent and hoisted her over his shoulder. He ran into the kitchen, bellowing loudly for Avery.

Avery, her hands covered in flour, looked up from where she and Leta were rolling out dough.

"Jeffrey? What's wrong?"

She watched as Jeffrey dropped Renee onto the table with a loud thump. Renee winced and reached underneath her to rub at her ass as Jeffrey grabbed Avery's arm.

"My lady! Renee has been burned. You must look at her. Please!"

"Of course!" Avery ran to the table as Leta hurried after her.

"It is her feet and her legs. I spilled hot water on them. I am such an idiot! Please, my lady you must hurry!" Jeffrey was nearly shouting with panic.

"Jeffrey! I'm fine, calm down," Renee said. "It is not that bad. I do not need Avery to look at -"

She was nearly pulled from the table when Jeffrey grabbed her shoes and yanked them off. He peeled off her socks and shoved up her pant legs as Avery reached for her right foot. She held it in her hand and scanned Renee's foot and leg anxiously.

She frowned. "It seems fine to me. Perhaps a little red, but it's not blistering."

"I told you, my lady, it's perfectly fine. I don't need -"

"Check her other leg!" Jeffrey was pacing back and forth next to the table and he gave Renee another frantic look. "I will never forgive myself if I have scarred even one small inch of your perfect skin!"

Renee blinked at him, her mouth dropping open as Leta climbed up on top of the table beside her. She peered curiously at Renee's feet as Avery, a small smile playing on her lips, took Renee's other foot in her hand. She held it lightly, the flour on her hands sucking up the moisture and creating a sticky mess on her hands and Renee's feet, before glancing at Jeffrey.

"Jeffrey," she said in a loud voice.

"Aye, my lady?" Jeffrey stopped his pacing and stared at her. "Is it bad? Can you not heal her?"

"She's fine. Could you be a dear and run to Renee's room and grab some clean socks for her? And perhaps a towel to dry her feet?"

"Aye, of course." Jeffrey gave Renee an anxious look. "Do not move, Renee. I will return shortly."

"It is the third room on the right," she called as Jeffrey disappeared down the hallway.

"Aye, I know!"

Leta squirmed under Renee's arm and stared at Jeffrey's stocky body running down the hallway. Renee squeezed the young Lycan's shoulders and kissed her forehead as Avery wiped the paste-like flour from Renee's feet.

"He likes you," Leta said. "I can smell it."

Avery snickered. "One does not have to be a Lycan to know he likes her, sweet Leta."

"Do you like him?" Leta asked Renee.

"I – well, I don't know. I mean, I've known him forever," Renee replied.

"He's liked you forever." Leta rolled her eyes before lying on her back on the table. She stared at the ceiling. "You should marry him."

"Leta, get off the table please," Avery scolded gently.

"Renee's on the table," Leta pointed out.

"Leta." Avery gave her a stern look and Leta, a small pout crossing her face, slid off the table and collapsed dramatically to the floor.

"I never get to do anything fun."

Avery ignored her and smiled at Renee. "He is very fond of you, Renee."

Renee blushed. "I – I had no idea."

Jeffrey came hurrying back into the kitchen. He had a towel in one hand but no socks. "I'm sorry. I did not know which drawer your socks were in and I did not want to rifle through your personal belongings," he said.

"It's fine, Jeffrey." Renee smiled at him. "I need to change my pants anyway."

She started to slide off the table and made another squeak of surprise when Jeffrey scooped her up.

"You should not be walking on your feet. You should probably rest them for a bit. I will carry you to your room," he said.

She blushed. "Thank you. That is very kind of you."

Leta popped up from the floor. "Her feet don't hurt any more, Jeffrey. Mama healed them, remember? She can walk just fine."

"Hush, Leta," Avery muttered as both Jeffrey and Renee flushed.

"It's probably better to be on the safe side." He cleared his throat as Renee put her arm around his shoulders and he carried her out of the kitchen.

Leta watched them leave before turning to her mother. "Why do grown-ups act so silly when they like someone?"

Avery laughed. "I don't know, my love. Come, let us finish making the pie."

CHAPTER 6

"**M**arian, watch out!" Dani hurried down the hallway and grabbed the plump woman. Marian, carrying a stack of laundry taller than her, was about to step on one of Leta's abandoned toys.

"Thank you, Dani." Marian smiled at her from around the laundry.

"Can I help you with these?"

"Aye, that would be nice."

Dani carefully took a stack of laundry from the towering pile. "Who do these belong to?"

"Those are Andric's," Marian replied. "He's such a sweet boy. He told me I didn't have to do his laundry, that he would do it himself, but I told him it made no difference to me. I was doing everyone else's. What does it matter if there's a bit more?"

She indicated to the shirt that was on the top of her pile. "This one is his, as well."

Dani took it and added it to the stack in her arms as Marian carefully stepped around Leta's toy. "He speaks so politely and has a very sweet manner, does he not?"

"I hadn't really noticed," Dani replied. She thought back to the things that Andric had said to her, to the way he had spanked her in the barn and then touched her while her mother was right there. Polite, she decided, was not the word she would use to describe Andric.

"Of course, you haven't," Marian said cheekily. "Will you take those to his room for me?"

"Of course." Dani gave her an embarrassed grin and quickly made her way to Andric's room. The door was ajar, and she knocked before entering the room.

"Andric? Are you here?" She was fairly certain he wasn't and that he was still outside with her brother and her cousin. She placed the clothes carefully on the bed. He hadn't made it this morning and she eyed the rumpled sheets with more than a little passing interest before sighing. She was being foolish.

She started across the room and then hesitated. Andric's bag was sitting on a chair beside the bed and she glanced around before walking toward it. She paused, warring with herself, before peeking into it. There wasn't much in it, most of his clothes were on the bed, and she reached in and pulled out a folded-up piece of paper that was nearly hidden under a pair of his socks. She unfolded it carefully, staring curiously at the drawing. It was of a man and a woman and she studied the man's face. Andric's father, she decided. The resemblance to Andric was very strong. The man had his arm around the woman, and she was smiling up at him.

Dani smiled a little. It was a nice drawing. It was smudged and a bit worn, she wondered how often Andric took the paper out to look at. He must miss them, she thought. Her heart suddenly hurt for him and for his loss. She couldn't imagine what it would be like to lose her mother and father in such a horrifying way. She folded up the paper and placed it carefully back in the bag, suddenly ashamed at her behaviour. She was curious about Andric, but it did not give her the right to snoop through his personal belongings.

"What are you doing?"

She jumped and spun around. Andric was standing in the doorway and he frowned at her as he entered the room and shut the door behind him.

"I'm sorry. I – Marian was carrying your laundry and there was a lot of it and so I offered to help and I, uh, I brought your laundry in." She pointed to the stack of laundry on his bed.

"Why were you looking through my bag?" He walked toward her, and she took a nervous step back.

"I wasn't."

He gave her a dry look. "You were."

"I'm sorry," she whispered.

He crossed his arms and stared thoughtfully at her. "I didn't take you for a snoop, Danielle."

"I'm not!" she protested. "I was just -"

"Just looking through my bag?"

She flushed and looked down at the floor as he stepped closer to her. "Do your parents know that you like to snoop through their guest's belongings?"

She shook her head. She was absolutely mortified, and she wished for a moment that the floor would open up and swallow her whole.

"I suppose they would be disappointed in you, if they knew."

"I'm sorry, Andric. It was rude of me to look through your things and I promise I won't do it again," Danielle said.

He nodded. "Aye, I believe you."

She smiled at him apologetically and started for the door.

"It does not mean that you shouldn't be punished, Danielle."

She stopped as a weird combination of dread and desire started up in her belly. "What do you mean?"

"I will give you a choice. You can be spanked by me, or I will speak with your parents about your rudeness and they can deal with it."

"What?" Dani stared at him, the blood draining from her cheeks.

Andric's look was stern. "You heard me, Danielle. You have a choice to make. Either you accept a spanking from me, or I speak with your family about your snooping."

Dani stared at the floor. Shame was spreading through her at the thought that Andric would speak to her parents like she was a small child.

"I'm sorry, Andric," she said. "I did not mean to -"

"You did mean to, Danielle. Do not make it worse by lying to me."

She sighed. "I am sorry."

"Aye, I know. Make your choice."

She made herself look at him. He was staring silently at her and she realized with dismay that he was completely serious. If she did not allow him to spank her, he would go to her parents. She would be treated like a child by her parents and –

And being spanked isn't being treated like a child?

She stared at the floor again. Not when it was Andric spanking her. Already her core was starting to ache, and she could feel her thighs trembling at the thought of lying across his lap, of his hard hand touching her ass. Andric inhaled deeply before grinning at her and sitting down on the bed.

"Come over here, Danielle."

"I haven't made my decision yet," she said.

"Have you not?" He inhaled again, his grin widening, and she flushed. She knew he could smell her desire and she closed her eyes briefly before walking toward him.

She stood next to the bed, her fingers twisting at her skirt as he smiled up at her. "Lift your skirt to your waist and lie across my lap, Danielle."

She gave him a dirty look. "This is ridiculous. Spanking me for snooping is silly."

He shrugged. "If you would prefer I speak to your parents, then I will. I'm sure they will be thrilled to know that their grown daughter is rifling through another's belongings."

She flushed and quickly lifted her skirt, bunching it around her waist before lying across Andric's lap. She could feel his firm thighs against her stomach, and she buried her face in the bed as he stared down at her ass.

"Lift your hips," he instructed.

She lifted them and made a soft squeal of surprise when he pulled her panties down to her knees. She reached for them and he pushed her hands away roughly before clamping one hard arm across her lower back. "No, Danielle. Keep your hands on the bed. If you disobey me, I'll add more spankings. Do you understand?"

"Aye," she muttered.

He caressed the back of her thighs and she twitched on his lap. There was a hardness pressing into her stomach and she realized with embarrassment and lust that it was his erection. He pressed down on her lower back, pushing her more firmly against his erection.

"Do you see what you do to me, Danielle?" he murmured. "I haven't even spanked you yet and already I'm hard."

"Your ass is amazing." He touched it lightly, making her moan. "So full and soft looking. I can't wait to spank it."

"Andric -"

"Hush, Danielle," he said. "I think ten spankings will do, don't you?"

She nodded, breathing a soft sigh of relief. She could

handle ten. He had spanked her before, and it hadn't hurt that badly. She could –

His hard hand came down, slapping her firmly across her bare ass, and she squealed with shock and pain.

"Hush, Danielle," he repeated. "Do you want the others to come in here and find you being spanked?"

She shook her head and buried her face in her arm as Andric spanked her again. She jumped and cried out into her arm. The spanking burned like fire and she could feel tears springing to her eyes. She had thought he would be gentle, had expected that he would spank her lightly, and she twisted and squirmed against him as he spanked her three more times in rapid succession.

He made a low growl of pleasure. "Your ass is red from my hand, Danielle. It looks so pretty. Look at it."

She shook her head. He threaded his fingers into her hair, pulling firmly until she looked over her shoulder at her ass. She could see red handprints on the pale flesh of her ass, and another wave of lust and shame went through her.

"Gods, your ass was meant to be spanked by me," Andric muttered. He released his grip on her hair and spanked her again. She scrambled to get away from him. Her ass was burning, and the flesh felt bruised and raw. She couldn't take another five more.

"Stop, Danielle. We're only halfway done."

"Please," she said breathlessly, as tears dripped down her cheeks. "I can't take anymore."

She gave him a hopeful, pleading look and he smiled at her as he rubbed her lower back. "You can. Besides, you should have thought of that before you went snooping through my things."

He slapped her again, the sound echoing in the small

room, and she made a thin cry of pain as her back arched. "Please, Andric."

"You're doing so well, Danielle," he said soothingly. "You're being such a good girl. Only four more and then we're done."

She buried her face back into the covers and bit down on to the soft quilt to muffle her cries as he slowly and methodically spanked her four more times. She collapsed against him, her ass burning and throbbing, and her body filled with a weird combination of lust and shame. He eased out from under her before lying down on his side next to her.

"Are you all right, Danielle?" He rubbed one thigh.

"What do you think?" She twisted her head to glare at him. "My ass is on fire!"

He smiled. "It is rather red. Did you enjoy your spanking?"

She gaped at him. "Did I - of course I didn't enjoy it! It was painful and humiliating and -"

"Are you sure?" he said.

"Aye, I'm sure! I -"

She broke off into a low moan when Andric unexpectedly pushed his hand between her thighs. He rubbed gently and then brought his hand up and showed it to her. His fingers were dripping with moisture and she turned bright red. For the first time, she became aware of how much her pussy was tingling and of the wetness dripping down her thighs.

His hand dipped between her legs again and she moaned when he rubbed her swollen, throbbing clit. She spread her thighs eagerly as he kissed her hard on the mouth and continued to rub her clit.

"Gods," she moaned again.

She reached for his cock, rubbing at it through his pants, and he made a low growl of need. She turned to her side and he cupped her breast through her shirt. He pinched her nipple and she arched her back before squeezing his erection. He groaned, and she reached for the button on his pants. Before she could undo it, he was pushing her hand away and sitting up on the side of the bed.

Her cheeks flushed and her body trembling, she hurriedly pulled up her panties and pushed down her skirt. She slid to the edge of the bed, wincing a little at the pain in her ass, and stared nervously at him.

He was staring at his tightly-clenched fists, his nostrils flared and his chest heaving rapidly. She touched his shoulder. "Andric? Did I do something wrong?"

He shook his head. "No, but you need to leave."

"Why?" Hurt flooded through her. She didn't want to go. She wanted to stay in Andric's bed. She wanted him to take away the aching and throbbing between her legs. She would go mad if he didn't.

He sighed harshly. "Just – just trust me on this, Danielle. You should go before I do something I regret."

"Like what?"

He gripped his legs. "Like taking your innocence."

She touched his shoulder again. "I want you to, Andric."

He stared at her, his eyes glowing, and she swallowed nervously. "I mean, if – if you want it, it's yours."

"And what of Kaden?" he asked. "Do you not wish to give that gift to him?"

"Kaden doesn't want it," she muttered. "Besides, you are right - I do want you. Why should I not give it to you? You would take this gift. Would you not?"

He swallowed hard. "Aye, I would."

She fit her slender body against his and pressed her mouth to the thick column of his neck. "Then take it."

"Danielle," he breathed, "you don't know what you're saying."

She frowned at him. "Of course, I do. I'm not a child."

"I know. But you are too sweet for me. It would not -"

"Stop saying that!" She blew her breath out in an angry rush. "I'm so tired of hearing about how sweet I am."

She reached out and gripped his still-hard cock. He groaned when she rubbed it through his pants. "I want you, Andric. It's not fair of you to – to make me want you this much, and then leave me to suffer. I can't sleep. I can't concentrate. It aches between my legs all the time now, and I don't know how to make it stop!"

He caught her hand and lifted it away before kissing the palm of it. "I am sorry, Danielle. You're right – it isn't fair of me. I will not touch you again."

Her stomach dropped and she ripped her hand away from him. "That isn't what I meant, and you know it!"

When he only looked at her apologetically, she lost her temper. She stood and glared at him. "You're an ass, Andric! Do you know that? A complete horse's ass! You know what I think? I think you have no idea how to please a woman and that's why you keep stopping. Maybe – maybe you're too innocent for me!"

She stomped toward the door. "That's fine. I'll find someone else to please me. Someone who knows how to bring a woman satisfaction and not just -"

She squeaked in surprise when she was pushed up against the door. Andric, his breath hot on her neck, ground his cock against her still-throbbing ass. "You should not try and goad me into fucking you, Danielle. It will not work."

"I'm not trying to goad you into anything," she snapped. "I wouldn't want someone who doesn't know what they're doing, taking my virginity."

He growled and, before she realized what he was doing, he had pulled her away from the door, stuck his hand down her skirt and panties and cupped her pussy. "If you think I won't spank you again for your impertinence, you're wrong," he warned.

She scoffed. "Aye, you're very good at spanking, aren't you? It's making a woman come that you find difficult."

She was embarrassed by her own crudeness, but she couldn't seem to stop. She was angry and frustrated and so turned on that she wanted to scream. It was all Andric's fault and she wanted to make him feel as badly as she did.

"Don't worry, Andric. I'm sure there's bound to be a woman out there who will be happy enough with just a spanking. Not every woman needs a real man to -"

Her words died in her throat when he growled and, using his left hand, tore the front of her blouse open. He cupped one naked breast roughly, his fingers pulling and squeezing her nipple until she gasped, and bit down onto her neck. His fangs had come out and she could feel them pressing against her soft skin. Another moan of need escaped her throat. She wanted him to bite her, wanted to feel that sharp sting of pain as he tasted her. It was not the full moon, there was no worry about him turning her, and she angled her head so her neck was bared fully to him.

He made another muffled growl before pulling his mouth away. He licked the indents left in her soft flesh from his fangs as his right hand moved between her thighs. His fingers parted the lips of her pussy and stroked roughly at her clit. Warmth burst in her belly and she wriggled against him as he rubbed harder.

"Andric, please," she begged.

He pulled again on one taut nipple, rolling it between his fingers as he continued to rub and stroke her throbbing clit.

Her breath was coming in hard, short gasps, and she rubbed her ass against his hard cock.

Her body tensed as a weird sensation built in her belly. She could feel her body stiffening, could feel her nipples becoming hard as glass and her clit swelling against Andric's rough fingers, and she stared at him over her shoulder. "Andric, what – what's happening? I can't -"

She arched her back, her words turning into a loud, inarticulate cry that was muffled when Andric slammed his mouth down on to hers. Pleasure flooded through her, radiating from her core to the rest of her body, as his fingers continued their relentless rubbing until she was weak and limp and trembling against him.

He held her up against the door as she caught her breath. She could feel his cock pressed firmly between her ass cheeks as she panted and shook and tried to calm her racing heart. She twitched when he grabbed her ripped shirt, but he only wrapped it around her, taking her hand and closing it around the two pieces to keep them shut.

He stepped back and she turned to look at him. "Andric, I -"

"Go, Danielle." He backed away as she dropped her gaze to the front of his pants. His cock was straining against the fabric and she took a step towards him.

"Let me -"

"No!" He gave her a look of anger and lust and pointed to the door. "Go right now!"

"Andric, let me -"

"Please," he said pleadingly.

Her face red and her body still trembling, she turned and fled.

CHAPTER 7

"Thank you for taking a walk with me, Bree," Danielle said as they stepped out the back door and into the cold sunshine.

"Aye, you're welcome." Bree took her hand and squeezed it. "It's a nice day for a walk and after that giant breakfast, I need some exercise."

She grinned at Dani before staring at the barn. There was a man talking to Marshall and Evan and she pointed at him. "Who is that man? Do you know?"

Danielle shrugged. "Not really. He looks a little familiar."

They watched as two other men came from the direction of the front of the house. They were cursing and sweating as they struggled to lead a bucking, prancing horse towards the barn.

"Are you sure the Lord Williams will want her?" One of the men shouted. "She's a wild one. We haven't been able to tame her at all in the last year."

Marshall nodded. "Aye, he'll take her. My brother enjoys a challenge."

Dani and Bree watched for a moment longer before

turning and heading toward the woods. Marshall looked their way. "Do not go too far into the woods, Danielle," he called.

"Aye, Dad. We will not." Dani waved at him and he winked at her before turning to help the men lead the horse into the barn.

As they walked through the woods, hand-in-hand, Danielle squeezed Bree's firmly. "Are you worried about James and Kaden?"

Bree shook her head. "I am not. I lived with Draken's pack for over two years. They are all cowards. Without Draken, they will fall easily. James and the others will be home soon. I know it."

Dani stepped over a fallen branch. The leaves crunched under their feet and she stared up at the sky for a moment. "It will snow soon."

"Aye," Bree agreed. "I hope it does not snow before the wedding. It will make it more difficult for your friends to join us."

"I can't believe James is getting married," Dani said. "It seems so strange."

"You do not seem to be as excited about the wedding, Dani. Is there something wrong?" Bree asked.

Dani shook her head. "No."

"Are you sure?"

"Aye." Dani was shocked to feel herself close to tears and she blinked them back rapidly as Bree tugged her to a stop.

"In my heart, I do not believe that Kaden will leave after the wedding," she said.

Dani shrugged. "What does it matter? He is in love with Sophia. Everyone knows it."

"I'm sorry," Bree replied. "I know you love him."

"Aye, I do." Dani hesitated. "At least, I thought I did."

"Perhaps you have found someone else whose company you enjoy more?" Bree said delicately.

Dani glanced at her and groaned. "Is it that obvious?"

"Aye. Although, it does not help that Leta goes around telling everyone that she can smell how much you and Andric like each other." Bree laughed.

Dani buried her face in her hands. "I'm going to kill that kid."

Bree laughed again and tugged her hands away from her face. "I told you – it is obvious even without Leta announcing it."

Dani suddenly burst into tears and Bree stared at her in bewilderment before hugging her. "Dani? What is wrong, my love?"

"Nothing – everything! I don't know!" Dani wailed. "I thought I was in love with Kaden and then Andric came along and gods, I want him so badly. Only he doesn't want me, just like Kaden does not, and I don't know what to do or what is wrong with me!"

Bree hugged her as Dani sobbed into her thin shoulder. "It's all right, Dani."

When Danielle's sobs had slowed to the occasional sniffle, Bree leaned back and wiped the tears from Dani's face with the heel of her hand. "How do you know that Andric does not want you? According to Leta and her super sense of smell, he does."

Dani sighed. "I offered him my virginity and he would not take it."

Bree blinked in surprise before giving her a cautious look. "Perhaps it is because he likes to move a bit more slowly."

Dani blushed. "We have done other things, Bree."

"Oh," Bree replied. "Well, I'm sure he has his reasons for –"

"He says I am too sweet for him. He says that he wants to do things to me that I would not enjoy," Dani said.

"What do you mean? Andric seems very polite and pretty sweet himself," Bree replied.

Dani blushed again. "He is not nearly as sweet as he appears, Bree. He says, um, very inappropriate things to me when we are alone."

Bree laughed. "Don't all men? James is the sweetest man I know, but he can say rather naughty things when we are in bed."

"It's not just what he says," Dani said carefully. "It is what he does."

"What does he do?" Bree asked.

Dani didn't reply and Bree patted her arm. "I'm sorry. It is none of my business. Come, we will walk a little further and -"

"He spanked me." Dani stared at the ground, her cheeks on fire, as the words came tumbling out of her. "He caught me snooping through his things and said I could make a choice between being spanked or having him tell my parents like I was a disobedient child. I chose the spanking. Earlier we had, well, we had made out in the barn and so I just jumped at the chance to have him touch me again, even if it was a spanking. He held me down on his lap and spanked me and even though it hurt, the whole time I could feel his – I could feel him pressing against my stomach and I liked what he was doing. I liked it a lot."

She paused for breath but didn't dare look up. "Afterwards, I – I asked him to take my virginity and he said no, and I got mad and told him that he probably didn't know how to even please a woman. And then that made him angry and he touched me until I," she paused, groping for the words and coming up empty, "until I, you know, and afterwards I wanted to return the favour but he would not let me. He made me leave. That was two days ago, and he's been avoiding me ever since."

She stopped, panting harshly and staring at the dead leaves under her feet. The seconds spun into minutes and, steeling herself for the look of horror in Bree's eyes, she raised her face to hers.

To her surprise, Bree was staring at her with a mixture of sympathy and mild amusement.

"What?" Dani asked.

"I had no idea you could speak that fast," Bree said.

"What's wrong with me, Bree? Andric says there are women who like this kind of thing, but I never thought I would. What does that say about me that I would enjoy being spanked like a small child?"

Bree took her arm and led her through the woods. "I think your enjoyment of it has less to do with being spanked and more to do with who is spanking you," she said.

"Gods. This is embarrassing," Dani groaned.

"There's nothing to be embarrassed about," Bree said.

"Is there not? So, you let James spank you then, do you?" Dani scoffed.

Bree shrugged. "I have not but if James wanted to try it, I would agree to it."

Dani blinked at her. "You would?"

"Aye, why not? Although just between you and I – I think I'd prefer to be the spanker rather than the spankee. I bet James would let me try it. He is agreeable to all sorts of things in bed."

Dani gaped at her and then burst into giggles. "I do not need to know that about my cousin, Bree."

Bree laughed. "Aye, perhaps not."

She stopped and squeezed Dani's arm gently. "Listen, I

am probably not the right person to talk to about this as I do not have very much experience myself. James is the only man I have been with, but I truly do not believe this is something to be embarrassed about. If both you and Andric enjoy it, where is the harm in it? Whatever the two of you do in bed together is your business, not anyone else's."

"Do you really mean that?" Dani asked.

"Aye, I do," Bree said. "And now I know why you keep wincing when you sit down."

Dani flushed bright red. "Gods be damned! Do you think anyone else has noticed?"

"I don't know. You should casually hug Mama today," Bree suggested. "Although she might become suspicious if you keep hugging her."

Dani giggled as an image of her sneakily hugging Avery every time Andric spanked her, popped into her head. She sobered abruptly and shook her head. "It's not nearly as sore as it was. Besides, Andric has made it clear that he will not touch me again."

She sighed. "Why do I keep choosing men who want nothing to do with me? Am I that much of a silly little girl?"

Bree frowned. "Andric wants you, Danielle. You just have to convince him that you are not as sweet as you appear. Perhaps you could be waiting for him in his bed? That's what I did with James."

Dani jerked in surprise. "You did not!"

"Aye, I did," Bree replied. "Of course, when Martine showed up to James' room in just her night dress, it got a bit awkward."

Dani shook her head. "I used to think you were so sweet, Bree."

Bree grinned. "I am sweet. Just like you."

She hooked her arm through Danielle's and led her back

toward the house. "Come, sweet Dani. Let us plot ways for you to win Andric's," she paused and stared at Dani with raised eyebrows, "heart?"

Dani laughed. "Is it awful if I say it's not his heart I am interested in at the moment?"

Bree snickered. "Absolutely not."

"DORAN? IT'S NEARLY SUPPER TIME." DANI STUCK HER HEAD into the barn. "Mama asked me to tell you and Evan and Andric to come in."

She stooped and petted the purring Hudson who was winding around her legs. "Where is Andric?"

Doran shrugged. "He went for a run in the woods. He said he would not be gone long."

"I'm going to go look for him," she replied.

Doran frowned. "You should not go into the woods alone, Dani."

"I won't go far."

"Dani -"

"You are not the boss of me, Doran," Dani said before leaving the barn.

She walked quickly through the trees. There was no sign of Andric and she sighed before leaning against a large oak tree. It was foolish of her to look for him. Despite what Bree had told her earlier, she knew she would never have the guts to keep throwing herself at him. She needed to accept that he might want her, but he would not take her the way she wanted him to. She was being pathetic.

A strong wind was blowing, and she shivered inside her jacket. She might as well go back to the warmth of the house. Andric would come back when he was ready and she –

She paused as there was movement in the bushes ahead of her. She ducked behind the tree and peered around it as Andric in his wolf form, came strolling out of the bushes. She trailed after him as he picked his way through the trees to another large oak tree. His clothes were piled at the base of it and he stopped and shifted to his human form. She stared at his naked ass as he bent and picked up his pants from the base of the tree. He slipped into them and she watched as, instead of buttoning them, he hesitated and then leaned against the tree with his back to her.

She stared curiously as he reached into his pants. His arm moved in a firm up and down motion and her face coloured when she realized abruptly what he was doing. He moaned and the motion of his arm increased as she stepped away from the tree.

You should not be watching this. Turn around and go back to the house before he catches your scent, she told herself.

Instead of leaving, she drifted closer, fascinated by the sounds of his soft moans and gasps. A gust of wind rattled through the trees, blowing her long hair around her face, and he stiffened. His head came up and he inhaled before he cursed under his breath.

"Go away, Danielle," he said roughly, without turning around.

Instead of doing what he asked, she moved up behind him and peered around his half-naked body. She inhaled sharply at the sight of his cock. He was holding the base of it in his hand and she stared unabashedly at the hard length of it.

"Danielle, go away. Please," he said.

"Please let me stay." She touched his naked back. It was warm, despite the cold, and she smiled to herself when his breath hissed out between his teeth. "Touch yourself, Andric. I want to watch."

He groaned and then stroked his hard cock with one rough hand. She watched as a drop of liquid formed at the tip before letting her gaze drift to the patch of light brown hair at the base of it.

"Does that feel good, Andric?"

"Aye," he gritted out.

She stroked his back, running her fingers over his smooth skin as his hand moved harder and faster over his cock.

"I want to touch it," she whispered.

"Of course, you do," he croaked in defeat. "You need to leave, Danielle. You -"

"Please, may I touch it just once? I have never touched one before," she said sweetly before placing a soft kiss on his shoulder.

He groaned and his left hand dug into the bark of the tree. "Just once."

"Thank you, Andric." She kissed his shoulder again and reached around him with a shaky hand. He dropped his right hand and she wrapped her fingers around him, squeezing firmly. His hips jerked in her hand and she let go immediately. "I'm sorry. Did that hurt?"

"No," he grunted.

He gasped when she touched him again, stroking the length of him with the tips of her fingers before curling her hand around the base. She moved her hand back and forth, stroking lightly then firmly, as he moaned and thrust his hips back and forth.

"Do you like that, Andric?" she whispered.

"Aye, I do," he moaned.

"Good," she murmured. She moved to his side and used her left hand to quickly unbutton her jacket and her shirt before taking his right hand and guiding it to her breast. He cupped it, running his thumb over her nipple as she squeezed and stroked his cock.

"Please, Danielle. You need to stop. I'm going to come if you don't," he groaned.

"I want you to," she breathed into his ear. "I want to watch you come. Please let me."

"Danielle," he whispered as she stroked him harder and faster.

"Kiss me, Andric."

He dropped his mouth to hers and kissed her frantically as she rubbed him. His cock was swelling in her hand, she could feel it, and she tore her mouth from his and watched as his back arched and he came in her hand. He threw his arm across his mouth to muffle his loud cry. Warm liquid poured from the tip of his cock and she ran her thumb through it before bringing it to her mouth and tasting it curiously. Andric, his eyes glowing brightly and a thick beard on his face, groaned as he watched her thumb disappear into her mouth.

"It tastes good," she said.

"Gods!" He groaned again before pushing her back against the tree. He kissed her fiercely, his tongue plunging deep within her mouth as both hands cupped and kneaded at her naked breasts. She sighed and thrust her pelvis against him.

"Touch me, please," she whimpered.

He was sliding his hand into her pants when he suddenly stopped and raised his head.

"What is it?" she whispered.

"Your twin," he muttered.

"The gods be damned!" She pushed at his naked chest and he stepped back as she hurriedly buttoned her shirt and jacket.

"Danielle!" Doran called.

"I'll be right there!" she shouted. She hurried toward the sound of her brother's voice as Andric slipped into his shirt and his boots. She gave him a quick, trembling smile before disappearing into the trees.

"Why is your mouth red?" Doran asked when she joined him.

"It isn't," she said.

"It is. It's -"

He stopped and sniffed at her before a weird look came over his face. "Oh gross," he muttered. "I can smell Andric's scent on you. Were you two making out in the woods?" He made another face. "Dad's going to kill him."

"Shut up!" she said. "It will have disappeared by the time we get back to the house."

Doran rolled his eyes. "You'd better hope so."

CHAPTER 8

D ani brushed her hair back from her face and, grunting loudly, shoved the stack of chairs to the side of the small storage room. Avery had needed some boxes moved to the storage room and Dani had volunteered to do it. She'd been anxious to get away from her father's gaze for even a few minutes. Dinner was incredibly uncomfortable. She'd sat as far away from him as she could but it hadn't even been a few minutes before her father was inhaling deeply, his eyes widening as he looked first at her and then Andric.

Dani sent a silent prayer of relief to the gods when her father started to stand and Maya grabbed his arm and tugged him back into his seat. He opened his mouth to speak and her mother shook her head before handing him the platter of duck.

She'd snuck a quick look at Andric. He was sitting beside her grandmother, smiling and teasing her gently, and hadn't appeared to even notice her father's actions. She'd said another silent prayer of relief. It was bad enough that practically her entire family knew what she and Andric were doing.

She couldn't imagine the embarrassment if her father actually said something to Andric.

Now, she lifted the heavy box and struggled to place it on the wooden shelving that ran across the left side of the room. She grunted again with madly shaking arms heaved it toward the top shelf.

She screamed breathlessly when Andric's arms circled around her. He took the box and easily placed it on the shelf. She turned and gave him a nervous smile.

"Thank you."

"Aye, you are welcome." He grinned down at her and she blushed furiously.

For some odd reason, she was feeling shy and nervous. The moment in the forest seemed almost like a dream and she could hardly believe that she had been that bold. She wasn't shy, but there was a difference between being outgoing and asking a man if she could touch his cock, she decided.

"You didn't eat very much at dinner," Andric said.

"I – I wasn't very hungry."

"No?" He raised his eyebrow at her. "Perhaps your father's obvious disapproval took away your appetite?"

She blushed again. "I don't know what you're talking about."

He laughed. "Oh really? So, I was imagining the murderous looks he was sending my way during dinner?"

"He wasn't. He doesn't know that I – that we..."

Andric laughed again and stepped closer, placing his hands on the shelving behind her and trapping her between them and his body. He leaned down, and she shivered when his warm breath tickled her ear. "He knows, Danielle. He can smell me all over you. All of the Lycans can."

She groaned with embarrassment. "This is so humiliating."

"Why? I like smelling my scent on you. I like that other Lycans know you belong to me."

A curious little shiver went down her back. She had always hated the Lycan's jealous nature, had sworn she would never be with someone who acted like she was a possession. So why did Andric's words make her nipples tighten and her core throb?

"Besides, it's your fault my scent is all over you. You were the one who insisted on touching my cock with your soft, little hand," he murmured into her ear.

She wanted to deny it but what was the point? It was the truth. "I have never touched one before. You can't blame me for being curious."

"Aye, I cannot," he replied. "Do you have any idea how much I like that my cock is the only one you've touched, Danielle? Did you like touching it?"

"Aye, I did," she whispered. She stared up at Andric. His eyes were a dark yellow and they were glowing softly in the dim light of the storage room.

"Did you like it?" she asked hesitantly.

"Very much so," he replied. "The way your hand looked wrapped around my cock is all I can think about, in fact."

His fingers traced the waistband of her pants and she gave him another nervous look. "What – what are you doing?"

"We were interrupted earlier. Remember? I never got the chance to do what you so sweetly asked of me."

She shuddered against him when he eased one finger inside her pants and traced a circle around her navel. "We cannot, Andric. My family is in the common room. My father knows I'm in here. He will come looking for me."

"Then we'd better hurry." Andric grinned wickedly at her before popping open the buttons one by one on her pants.

"Spread your legs." He kissed her mouth.

She shifted her legs apart, her hands digging into his arms when he slid his hand into her pants and underwear. He palmed her pussy, his fingers stroking the soft hair, as she moaned loudly.

"Shh, my sweet," he whispered. He kissed her again, his lips pulling lightly at her bottom lip, and she pressed her body against his hard one. He slid his other hand to her ass and squeezed it tightly through her clothing. "How is your ass, my sweet? Still sore?"

She shook her head as he slipped his free hand beneath her pants and rubbed her naked ass. "Your ass is so amazing," he muttered almost to himself.

"Andric, please," she moaned.

His fingers finally touched her aching clit and she thrust her pelvis at him as warmth surged through her belly. He used the tips of his fingers to rub it in small circular motions before he pinched it lightly.

"Oh!" Her eyes popped open and she stared at him. He smiled and kissed the tip of her nose.

"Tomorrow I want you to go without panties," he said.

"What?" She blinked at him.

"I don't want you wearing panties tomorrow, Danielle." He stroked her clit roughly and her fingernails dug into his arms.

"I – I can't go without panties!" she said.

"You can and you will." He squeezed her ass again. "At some point tomorrow, I'll check to see that you've obeyed me. If you haven't," his hand slid up and down her ass, "I'll spank you."

Wetness gushed between her legs, unstoppable and uncontrollable, and he grinned knowingly at her. He moved his hand lower and slid his index finger into her warm opening. She moaned and the smile dropped from his face as he felt her tighten around his finger.

"Gods, Danielle," he muttered. "You have no idea what you do to me."

She panted and moaned again in reply and he used his thumb to rub her clit roughly as he slid his finger in and out of her. She stiffened against him before making a small bird-like cry of pleasure and burying her face into his thick neck. She came violently, her slender body shaking wildly, and he pressed his erection against her as he continued to rub her clit.

When she had slumped against him, he pulled his hand from the front of her pants. His fingers were dripping with moisture and she felt another sharp pang of arousal when he slid the index one into his mouth.

"You taste very sweet, Danielle," he whispered.

"Come back to my room," she pleaded. "I want you in my bed, Andric."

Before he could reply, they heard the sound of Marshall's voice in the hallway. She stared at him in wide-eyed horror and he grinned and put his finger to his mouth in a shushing gesture.

"Is she that bad, Leo?"

"Aye, Marshall. The mare is a wild one. She might be too much for even Tristan to tame."

"My brother has a way with horses. If anyone can tame her, it will be him."

"Perhaps you're right."

Danielle breathed a sigh of relief when her father and Leo's voices faded down the hallway. Andric squeezed her ass a final time before buttoning her pants quickly.

"Good night, Danielle. Remember – no panties tomorrow." He kissed her again and she frowned at him.

"Andric, will you not join me in my bed?"

He shook his head with regret. "Not tonight, sweet one."

She sighed with frustration as he reached for the door and opened it. He ushered her into the hallway, and she turned to him. She wrapped her arms around his waist and trailed kisses down his neck.

"I want you to join me in my bed." She hoped she sounded seductive. "There are many things you could teach me and I -"

"Danielle!" he said loudly, and she glanced up at him. He was looking over her shoulder and she whirled around. Vivian was standing behind them and Danielle turned a brilliant, crimson red as her grandmother grinned.

"Hello, Andric. Hello, Danielle."

"Good evening, Mrs. Williams," Andric said as Danielle muttered a hello and stared at her feet.

There was a moment of awkward silence and then Andric lifted Danielle's hand to his mouth. He kissed the knuckles gently. "Good night, Danielle."

He nodded to Vivian. "Mrs. Williams."

"Andric."

He disappeared down the hallway as Danielle continued to stare at her feet. She hoped that her grandmother would follow him.

"Are you going to stare at your feet forever, Danielle?" Vivian asked.

"No." Danielle made herself look at her grandmother. "Grandmamma, nothing happened with Andric. He was just helping me put the boxes in the storage room and -"

"Oh please, Danielle," Vivian laughed. "I may be an old Lycan, but I can still remember what it was like to have a fire burning in your belly for another."

She held her hand out. "Come, walk me to my room."

"Please don't tell Dad," Danielle pleaded as she took Vivian's hand and they started down the hallway.

Vivian gave her a dry look. "I am quite confident he already knows."

"Do you like Andric, Grandmamma?"

"Aye, I do," she confirmed. "Has he told you what happened to his pack?"

Danielle shook her head. "No. He says it is not a story for someone as sweet as I am."

Vivian stared thoughtfully at her. "Perhaps he is right."

"I am not a child!" Danielle said. "Why does everyone treat me like one?"

"I believe it has less to do with thinking you're a child and more to do with wanting to protect you from the ugliness of the world," Vivian replied.

"I cannot be protected forever."

"Aye, I suppose not," Vivian agreed. "Do you love him?"

Danielle gave her a startled look. "I hardly know him. It's only been a week or so."

"True. But your mother fell in love with your father very quickly," Vivian said.

"I – I am in love with Kaden," Danielle replied.

"Are you now?" Vivian looked appraisingly at her. "Why?"

"What do you mean?"

"Why are you in love with him?" The old Lycan asked with a touch of impatience.

"Well, because he is strong and brave and handsome. He's kind despite everything that has happened to him."

"Andric is all of those things as well," Vivian pointed out.

"I don't know Andric very well and -"

"You don't know Kaden very well. Besides, he is -"

"In love with my cousin. I know," Danielle said.

They were at her grandmother's room and Vivian bent and kissed Danielle's forehead. "You are a smart girl, Danielle. You know in your heart that Kaden will never love you the way you believe you love him. Do not throw away the chance to find your happiness with Andric by carrying a useless torch for Kaden."

"Andric knows that I love Kaden and he does not seem to care. Where is the harm in having some fun with Andric? He is not in love with me nor I with him. Why should we not enjoy each other's company for a while? He will be leaving for Vanden when Kaden and the others return anyway," Danielle protested.

Vivian shook her head. "That does not make it right, Dani. You know that. Make your decision, girl. Will you pine for a man you can never have, or find out if there could be something deeper than 'having fun' with Andric?"

Danielle stared miserably at her and Vivian's expression softened. "I know this is not easy, child. But I trust you will make the right decision."

She kissed Dani's cheek and disappeared into her bedroom. Dani, sighing loudly, continued down the hall to her bedroom. She collapsed on her bed and stared up at the ceiling. Her stomach was churning and her mind whirling and although she knew her grandmother was right, she had no idea what to do.

CHAPTER 9

A ndric stood in the doorway of the kitchen and watched as Dani helped Nadine peel potatoes for supper. He inhaled, a small smile crossing his face when Dani's scent drifted to him. Gods, he wanted her. She was all he thought about and he let his gaze drift to her small, firm ass clad in tight pants. He wondered if she had done what he asked. She had been avoiding him all day and he was itching to check for himself if she had obeyed his order last night.

She laughed softly at something Nadine said to her and his smile widened in response. Despite what she said, she was very sweet and there was something about her that called to him in a way he had never felt before. The smile dropped from his face abruptly. She might want him, but she was in love with the human called Kaden, and he would be wise to shield his heart from her.

It's too late for that, and you know it.

He frowned. He was not in love with Danielle. He might be fonder of her than other women he had been with but that did not make it love. As soon as the others returned, he would continue to Vanden. His cousin and his family would welcome him, and he would be a part of a pack again.

His stomach clenched painfully. The loss of his parents and siblings, of his pack, weighed heavily on him and he wondered if that was one of the reasons he was so fond of both Danielle and her family. They were a close-knit pack, they reminded him strongly of his own pack, and it was not surprising that he wanted to be a part of it. It had been nearly two moons since the leeches had slaughtered his pack and for the first time since he had come home and discovered them dead, he was feeling a small thread of happiness. He had spent most of the first few weeks after their deaths, in his wolf form. He had roamed the forest, killing any leeches or fairies he stumbled on to, not caring if he lived or died, and believing he might go insane with the grief.

Although he wanted Danielle, wanted to feel her slender thighs wrapped around his waist as he made her his, it was his eagerness to be a part of a pack again that had made him so agreeable to staying with them, he decided. With the exception of Marshall, and Andric could hardly blame him for that, Danielle's pack had made him feel welcome without any hesitation. It had nothing to do with his delight at discovering Danielle's submissiveness, or his own eagerness to explore her body and have her explore his.

She is in love with another and your feelings run much deeper than you'll admit. You are not such a fool to believe that you can be with her and then leave, Andric. You would be wise to keep your distance from her. His father's dry voice spoke in his head and Andric felt another pang of loss.

Aye, it would be wise of him but, as he watched Nadine disappear down the hallway, he couldn't stop from walking quickly into the kitchen and pressing his body against Danielle's.

"Hello, Danielle." He stroked her side through her shirt, enjoying the way she shivered at his touch.

"Hello," she said.

"You've been avoiding me today."

"I haven't."

"Aye, you have." He kissed the side of her neck. "Is it because you have disobeyed me and are trying to avoid a spanking?"

She didn't reply but her fingers tightened on the counter and she pressed her ass against his erection when his hand moved to the waistband of her pants.

"No," she whispered. "I didn't – didn't wear any today."

He grinned. "I think it's best if I check for myself."

"Nadine will be right back," she said quickly. "There isn't time to -"

Her words died out in a soft little moan as Andric quickly pushed his hand into her pants. He cupped her bare pussy, tugging lightly on the hair, before touching her clit with his finger.

"Good girl, Danielle," he whispered into her ear before tracing it with his tongue. "You became so wet yesterday when I spoke of spanking you that I was certain you would disobey me just to be spanked again."

She didn't reply but her hips were thrusting rhythmically against his finger. He kept his hand still and licked her mouth when she turned her face toward him. "Do you like being spanked by me, Danielle?"

"You know I do," she muttered.

"Tell me."

"Do not make me say it."

He pinched her clit, making her gasp, and licked her mouth again. "Say it, Danielle."

"I like being spanked by you."

She moaned when he rewarded her with another few strokes of her clit. She was growing wetter by the second and he grinned at her.

"Perhaps you should come to my room tonight, Danielle. I'm sure I can find another reason to spank a good girl like you."

She stared at him. "Will you make love to me afterward, Andric?"

He hesitated and the desire on her face was replaced by anger. She yanked his hand from her pants and stepped away from him, wrapping her arms protectively around her torso.

"What is wrong with you?" she said with an angry huff. "What kind of man enjoys torturing a woman like you torture me?"

"You are not the only one being tortured, Danielle." He was suddenly as angry as she.

"And that is my fault?" she asked. "I have offered myself repeatedly to you, only to be turned down. I could hide naked in your bed and you would do nothing more than spank me before sending me on my way, is that not true?"

He didn't reply and she scowled at him. "Leave me be, Andric. If you are not going to take the gift I have offered you then I would rather you didn't touch me at all. I have no desire to be teased in such a manner."

"Aye, and I have no desire to take the precious gift you offer just so that you can close your eyes and pretend it's another man while I am between your legs," he growled.

Her face paled. "I would not do that."

"Would you not?" he asked. "You have made it perfectly clear that it is Kaden you love. Why would I not believe that you're using me as a substitute for the man you love?"

"Andric, you – you do not care that I am in love with him. You said so, yourself."

"I never said that, Danielle," he argued. He stepped forward and took her by the arms. "You have a decision to make. I will take you to my room right now and make love to you, if you can assure me that you are not in love with Kaden. Can you promise that it is me you want to be with and not him?"

She hesitated, and he cursed and released her before striding toward the doorway.

"Andric – wait! I -"

He shook his head. "No, you have made your decision. Enjoy your lonely bed."

He left the room, ignoring his urge to return to Danielle when he heard her burst into tears.

"THE GODS BE DAMNED!" LEO SHOUTED AS HE STRUGGLED TO control the wild horse. The horse was kicking and bucking, and Doran jumped out of the way, as one large hoof nearly connected with his ribs.

Cursing and sweating, Leo slowly gained control of the horse. Andric and Doran watched as he tried to lead her into an empty stall. The horse began to buck again, and Leo quickly tied her to the post of the stall, leaving her to stand in the wide aisle of the barn.

"Are you just going to leave her there all night, Leo?" Doran asked.

Leo shook his head. "No. I'll lure her into the stall with some oats. It's better than trying to force her into it."

He reached out and patted the horse's broad neck. She snorted and he drew his hand back quickly before giving Doran a look of satisfaction. "She's getting better."

Doran looked at him in disbelief and Leo nodded. "She

didn't try to bite me this time." He cautiously petted her again and smiled when the horse stood quietly. Her sides were heaving, and her body was slick with sweat but she made no objection when Leo ran his hand down her side.

"It's a good sign," he said before walking toward the far end of the barn to the barrel of oats.

"Uncle Tristan is going to have his hands full with that one," Doran said.

Andric snorted derisively. "A Lycan with a barn full of horses. Ridiculous."

"What's wrong with you? You've been in a foul mood for the last two days." Doran said.

"I haven't," Andric replied.

Doran rolled his eyes. "Whatever, Andric. Did you have a fight with my sister? She's been moping about and will hardly speak, and Dani never shuts up."

Andric frowned at him. "Do not speak that way about her."

Doran grinned at him. "She says worst things about me, trust me."

Before Andric could reply, the door to the barn opened and Dani walked in. She walked toward them, giving the horse in the aisle a wide berth, and stared at her brother. "Mama is looking for you."

"What does she want?"

"I don't know," Dani said irritably. "I didn't ask."

Her eyes flickered to Andric. He stared impassively at her and she coloured before clearing her throat. "Hello, Andric."

"Hello." He folded his arms across his chest and looked over her head as she bit at her lip before turning back to her brother.

"You'd better go."

"Aye, you are right. I want to go to town tomorrow and if

I am to convince her to let me go, I need to be on my best behaviour," Doran said with a laugh.

He turned to Andric. "Do you want to go with me, Andric? I could use the company."

Andric shook his head. "I am leaving tomorrow."

Dani gasped but he refused to look at her as Doran frowned at him. "Leaving?"

"Aye."

"You told Grandmamma you would stay until Uncle Tristan and the others returned," Dani said.

"I've changed my mind. I have lingered too long as it is. I must get to Vanden and find my cousin. I'll explain it to your grandmother, and I am sure she will understand."

"Andric, please don't," Dani hesitated and gave Doran a quick look before plunging forward, "don't leave because of me. I am sorry for what I said and did. I do not wish for you to leave with things the way they are between us."

Andric shrugged. "There is nothing to be sorry about, Danielle. I have enjoyed my time with you and your family, but I have stayed far longer than I anticipated."

"I don't want you to leave. I will miss you," she said.

"Do not worry. Your love will return soon enough, and you'll be otherwise occupied," Andric replied.

Her face very pale and her eyes swimming with tears, Dani turned and scurried away. Doran gave Andric a look of disgust. "Asshole," he muttered before hurrying after Dani. "Dani! Wait!"

She ignored him and walked faster as Hudson crept out of the empty stall that the wild mare was tied to. He sniffed the horse's front leg gingerly before rubbing up against it. The horse snorted in surprise and fear as its powerful back legs kicked back reflexively.

"Dani! Look out!" Doran screamed.

There was horrible muffled thud as the horse's back foot connected solidly with the side of Dani's head. She dropped to the floor of the barn like a stone and Doran screamed again, the sound of a wild animal caught in a trap, as he grabbed his sister and dragged her away from the horse.

"Dani! Dani!" He wailed as he cradled his sister in his arms. Andric fell to his knees beside him and stared in horror at Dani. A small section of her skull was caved in and he could see shards of bone sticking out as blood poured from the wound. Blood was trickling out of her ear and he stared helplessly at her as Leo came running toward them and pushed him out of the way.

He rested his hand on Dani's chest. "She still breathes. Doran, go and get Avery. Now!"

The young man stared blankly at him and Leo slapped him across the face. "Doran! Your aunt! Go quickly!" he roared.

Doran, his face the colour of rotting cheese, stood and ran from the barn screaming Avery's name. Andric staggered to his feet and backed away. He couldn't take his eyes from Dani's face, from the wound on her head or the blood that was pooling beneath her skull.

"No," he whispered. His hands reached up and tore at his hair as Leo stroked Dani's face.

"Stay with us, Dani," Leo whispered. "Hang on, sweet girl. Hang on."

There was a howl of panic and sorrow and Leo looked up as Andric, his face full of madness, shifted to his Lycan form. He lifted his head and howled deafeningly. Leo winced as all of the horses in the barn neighed loudly in fear and Andric howled again before fleeing the barn and disappearing into the forest.

CHAPTER 10

"You should be resting, dearest." Maya wrapped her arms around Dani's waist and kissed her cheek.

"I'm not tired," Dani said. She was standing at the window to her bedroom, staring out into the darkness.

"You need to rest," Maya repeated.

"How is Aunt Avery?" Dani asked.

"She's fine. She slept after healing you, and Laura and I rested with her."

"Are you sure she's all right?" Dani asked.

Maya nodded. "Positive."

She turned Dani around. "Look at me, my love." She examined Dani's head carefully, running her fingers over the side of it before studying her face.

"I don't know what I would have done if we had lost you," she whispered. Tears were starting to slide down her cheeks and Dani hugged her.

"I am fine, Mama. Aunt Avery got there in time and I feel perfectly normal."

"Your head does not hurt? Are you sure?" Maya asked.

"I am sure." Dani gave her a small smile. "For someone who almost died earlier, I am feeling remarkably well."

Maya cried harder. "Oh, Danielle."

Dani hugged her again and buried her face in her mother's neck. "I love you, Mama."

"I love you too. We all do. Your father and brother and -"

"Aye, I know." Dani smiled at her. "Both Dad and Doran have stopped in repeatedly to remind me that they love me. I had to practically push Doran out the door. His declarations of love were weirding me out."

Maya laughed through her tears. "I have a feeling it will be a long time before your twin lets you out of his sight."

"Aye, he does seem -"

She stiffened as there was a drawn-out howl from the forest. She untangled herself from Maya's grip and ran to the window, peering out into the darkness. Even through the window, she could hear the pain and sorrow in the howling, and she blinked back the tears as Maya joined her.

"I should be out there looking for him, Mama," she whispered.

There was another loud howl and this time it was joined by a chorus of howls from the wolves that lived in the forest. Goose bumps rose on Dani's flesh as Andric howled again and again. It was a desolate sound, one that made her want to cry.

"I need to go and find him. He believes I am dead," she said.

Maya squeezed her waist. "You cannot go and look for him. It is too cold and dark, and you need to rest, despite what you say."

"Mama -"

"Both your brother and your father tried to find Andric. Your brother could not find him at all, and your father said he saw him briefly, but Andric would not allow him to get close enough to tell him you were fine."

"Dad went looking for him?" Dani asked.

"Aye, he did," Maya said.

"Was he – was he all right?"

"Your father said he was not hurt."

Dani sighed miserably. "I'm so worried about him, Mama. He should not be alone in the forest. It's cold and there are creatures that would hurt him."

"He is a Lycan. He will be fine," Maya said. "And think of how happy he will be when he returns and sees you alive and well."

"What if – what if he does not return?" Dani said.

"He will. All of his things are still here. I would not be surprised if he has returned by the time we wake." Maya led Dani to her bed and helped her climb in. "Lie down and get some sleep, dearest. Would you like me to stay with you tonight?"

"No, Mama. I'm fine."

"Are you sure?"

"Aye. Thank you." Dani kissed her mother goodnight and smiled when Maya blew her another kiss before leaving her room. She laid in bed and stared up at the ceiling as howl after howl filled the night air. Each one was like a knife to her heart and after only a few moments, she climbed out of bed and went back to the window. She strained to see into the darkness, snorting with frustration and anger, before returning to her bed.

She paused, staring thoughtfully at her bed, before making a sudden decision. She opened the door to her bedroom and peered into the hallway. It was quiet and dark, and she slipped down the hall to Andric's room.

ANDRIC WALKED SILENTLY THROUGH THE DARK HOUSE. HE was naked and there was a long cut, already starting to heal, slashed across his chest. He stopped in front of Dani's bedroom door and clamped down fiercely on the howl that wanted to escape.

She was dead, just like everyone else he had ever loved, and he would never hear her voice or see her lovely face again. He felt the madness that had swallowed him in the barn trying to claw its way free again, and he moaned and gripped his head in his hands.

He had to leave. If he stayed here a moment longer with the memory of her and the ghost of her scent, he really would go mad.

He moved down the hallway to his room and entered it quietly before walking to his bag. He reached for his pants, dropping them and swinging around when her soft voice said, "Andric?"

He stared wide-eyed at her as she stood up from the bed and walked toward him. He backed up, bumping into the wall, as she drew closer.

"Are you a ghost?" His voice was raspy from howling.

"No." Her eyes dropped to his chest and she made a soft cry of dismay. "You're hurt."

She reached for his chest and he cringed back. "You were injured badly. The horse caved in your skull. I saw it – you are dead."

His eyes searched the side of her head as she smiled at him. "Do you remember when you saved me from the Gogmagog?"

He nodded, his hands trembling badly, as she stepped closer. "You were injured. Your ribs had punctured your lung and you collapsed. When you woke, only an hour later, you were healed."

"Aye," he whispered. "My Lycan healing powers -"

"No," she said. "It was not your healing powers, Andric. They could not have healed you so quickly. My aunt has a gift. She is a healer. She can touch people and heal them of their wounds. She held you while you were unconscious and healed your broken ribs and punctured lung."

"That is not possible," he whispered.

"It is, Andric. I promise you. She healed me earlier today. It is why I'm standing in front of you now," she said. "We keep my aunt's gift a secret. There are those who would seek to use it for their own gain if they knew about it. Do you understand why we didn't tell you?"

He nodded, his eyes scanning her head and face again. "You – you are not dead."

She smiled. "No. I am not."

When he continued to stare at her, she reached out and took his hand. She pressed it against her heart. "My heart beats, Andric."

"You are not dead," he whispered again before falling to his knees in front of her. He pressed his face into her flat stomach and wrapped his arms around her waist as she stroked his thick hair.

"I am so sorry, Danielle. I spoke cruelly to you and I did not mean it. I swear I did not." He looked up at her and she brushed her fingers across his forehead.

"Aye, I know. I'm sorry too, Andric."

"You have nothing to be sorry about," he said.

She tugged him to his feet. "I do. I treated you very badly and I feel awful about it."

He touched her head before staring at her apprehensively. "Does that hurt?"

"No. Aunt Avery healed me completely."

"Thank the gods," he whispered before pulling her into a bone-crushing hug. She wrapped her arms around him and buried her face into his neck, breathing deeply.

"I do not love Kaden," she said. "It is you that I care for. I want to be with you, Andric. I swear it."

He cupped her face and kissed her. "I want to be with you as well, Danielle."

She smiled at him and took his hand before leading him to the bed. "Will you join me in your bed?"

"Aye." He glanced at her head again. "Are you – are you sure that you are well enough?"

"Quite sure." She smiled at him. "We should clean your cut first though."

"It is already healing." He kissed her again, cupping her breast through her thin night dress and marveling at the rapid beat of her heart beneath it.

She moaned softly and stepped back. He watched as she gripped the hem of her night dress and pulled it from her body. She stood naked in front of him, dropping the night dress to the floor and smiling with satisfaction when his eyes roamed over her naked body and his cock hardened.

"Take me to bed," she whispered.

He took a deep breath and joined her as she climbed into his bed. She laid on her back and stared up at him as he traced her collarbone with the tips of his fingers. He bent his head and followed the path of his fingers with his tongue, and she moaned before pushing his head toward her breast. He captured her nipple in his mouth, sucking firmly on it as it tightened in his mouth, while his other hand stroked and kneaded her hip.

"Andric," she sighed his name as he lifted his head and kissed her hard on the mouth. Their tongues met, licking and sliding together, and he groaned into her mouth when her soft hand touched his erection. She stroked it firmly as he slipped his hand between her thighs and caressed the soft skin of her inner thigh.

"Please," she whispered.

He moved his fingers to her swollen clit. He rubbed it lightly as she arched her pelvis against him and the combination of his fingers and hot mouth quickly brought her to climax. He swallowed her loud cry with his mouth, and she collapsed against the bed, panting heavily, her hand still holding his cock.

He groaned when she ran her thumb over the head of it. Her other hand moved to his hip and pulled him toward her as she spread her legs and urged him between them.

"Danielle, are you sure?" he whispered.

"Aye. I want you to be my first, Andric." She kissed his mouth, licking and nipping at his lips. "I want you and only you."

He moaned and moved between her outstretched legs. His cock probed at her opening and she tensed before relaxing against the bed.

"Danielle..."

"Don't make me wait any longer," she said. "Please, I need you."

He hesitated and then pushed smoothly into her. She winced, a look of pain crossing her face for a moment, and he stared worriedly at her. "I'm sorry."

She ran her fingers over his jaw. "It only hurt a little."

Despite her assurances, he waited, even when she made small motions under him, her hips bumping against his. He gritted his teeth. He did not want to hurt her anymore than –

He yelped under his breath when she suddenly slapped him hard on the ass. He stared down at her and she giggled.

"I thought it was time you got a taste of your own medicine."

He growled teasingly at her and she squeezed his naked ass again. "If you don't fuck me, Andric, I'll spank you. I swear it."

"Naughty girl," he said before leaning down and kissing her. "Brace your feet on the bed, Danielle."

She did what he asked, and her hands slid around his waist as he propped himself above her. "Tell me if it hurts," he said.

"Aye," she said impatiently. "Please, Andric."

He thrust in and out of her, watching her face carefully. She smiled at him and met each of his thrusts as her hands gripped his waist tightly. She was very wet, and he groaned at the way her pussy clung to him. The tight, warm heat was driving him to the brink, and he slowed his thrusting. She frowned and panting lightly, whispered, "Don't stop, Andric."

He groaned and plunged in and out of her. She made soft cries of pleasure and he watched her small breasts bounce as he moved within her. Her face was flushed, and she was tossing her head back and forth as he increased the motion of his hips. He was reaching between them to rub her clit when she surprised him by suddenly climaxing. Her pussy tightened around him, trapping him inside of her, and he moaned hoarsely before coming deep within her.

"Gods!" she cried out. Her hands scratched at his back and she shuddered madly beneath him before he collapsed against her body.

He rolled off of her and immediately gathered her close. He kissed her face, her neck, and her mouth as she caught her breath. She opened her eyes and smiled hazily at him. "Is it always like that, Andric?"

He shook his head. "I have never felt anything like that before, Danielle. You were amazing."

She coloured prettily. "I bet you say that to all the girls."

"No. I have never cared for a woman the way that I care for you," he said. "When I thought you were dead, I wanted to die as well."

"Andric, I…"

"Am I scaring you, Danielle?" he asked.

"No. I just – you will be leaving for Vanden soon and I think it's better if we don't get too, uh, attached to each other," she said.

"I do not want to leave you, Danielle. Do not ask me to do so," he said.

She heaved a sigh of relief. "Truly?"

"Aye. I would stay with you for as long as you will have me."

She smiled delightedly at him and threw her arms around his neck. "I hope you're prepared to be here for a very long time."

CHAPTER 11

"Andric?"

"Aye?"

"Will you tell me what happened to your pack?" Dani rested her head on Andric's chest.

He sighed deeply and Dani lifted her head to stare at him. "If you do not wish to tell me because it is too painful for you, I'll understand. But if it's only because you wish to protect me, I would have you tell me what happened. I am not as fragile as you believe me to be."

He kissed her softly on the mouth. "Aye, I know."

He gently pushed her head back to his chest and stroked her back. He stayed quiet and she was just believing that he wouldn't tell her when he said, "Truthfully, I do not know exactly what happened. I had left the pack and was in a town called Morden."

"Why did you leave your pack?" she asked.

"I'd had a fight with my father. A stupid fight over the fact that I had no wish to settle down and mate with a female from our pack. I was the oldest of my siblings and my father believed I was setting a bad example for my younger siblings."

"Were you?"

"Aye, I suppose I was," he replied.

She kissed his chest and he squeezed her hip before continuing. "I spent two days in Morden, getting drunk and sleeping with any woman -"

He paused and Dani lifted her head and gave him a dry look. "I get the picture."

He actually blushed and a small smile crossed her face. "Go on."

"After two days I was missing my pack and ready to apologize to my father. Although I had no intention of mating with the female he had chosen for me, I was willing to be… better behaved, I guess you could say."

He sighed again and cleared his throat. "When I returned to my home, I discovered that most of my pack was dead or missing. It – it was horrifying. They had obviously put up a fight. There was ash and blood everywhere and some of my dead pack mates had terrible wounds that could only have been caused by a leech's bite."

She rubbed his chest soothingly as he took a deep, wavering breath. "My father was among the dead in the forest around our homes. I found my mother and three of my siblings dead in our home. Two of my brothers were among the missing."

His voice was so low she could barely hear him, and she kissed his warm skin repeatedly. "I'm so sorry, Andric."

He didn't reply and she glanced upward, tears slipping down her own cheeks when she saw the moisture on his face. She sat up and leaned over him, kissing him on his cheeks and his mouth, as she wiped gently at his face. "I'm sorry. I should not have made you tell me."

He shook his head. "It's fine. It actually feels better to talk about it."

She rested her forehead against his for a moment and then straightened. She rubbed her hands across his chest and abdomen as he stared up at the ceiling.

"Do you know why the leeches attacked?" she asked.

"No. Not really. I know that the leader of our pack had issues with both humans and leeches, but I do not believe he'd had any contact with either in many years. I don't understand why the leeches would attack our pack. Why they would kill some but take my brothers and the others."

"You couldn't find them?"

He shook his head. "By the time I returned to the pack, the leeches' scent and that of my pack mates had long faded. There were rumours in Morden of a large leech colony deep within the outskirts and I thought about trying to find it but I -"

He paused and she could almost feel the shame radiating from him. "I went a little crazy. I shifted to my Lycan form and spent the next few weeks in the forest."

She stroked his hair back from his face. "That's understandable, my love."

"When I finally returned to my senses, I realized that going to the leech colony by myself was a fool's plan. I would never defeat them and besides, I have no idea if my brothers were there or not. They were most likely dead. The leeches would have drained them within the first day or so of capturing them."

He stared up at the ceiling again. "I decided to go to Vanden to find my cousin. I knew he would welcome me into his pack, and there was a small part of me that thought I could convince him and some of the others to search for the leech colony."

99

"Andric – you would never survive. You know that," Danielle whispered. Cold fingers were tightening around her heart, and she swallowed down her panic at the thought of Andric leaving her.

He turned his gaze to hers. "The last words I spoke to my father were words of anger. I called him a foolish old man, and I will never forgive myself for that. While my pack mates were being slaughtered, I was drunk and wallowing in self-pity. I owe it to them to avenge their deaths."

She stared at him in sorrow and took his hands, squeezing them tight. "Your father knew you loved him. I am sure of it. And I do not believe he would want you to go on some suicide mission."

"Aye, perhaps not," he said.

Danielle, panic still clutching at her chest, cupped his face and turned it towards hers. "Andric, you said you would stay for as long as I wanted you to. Are you breaking that vow?"

He shook his head. "No, sweet Danielle. I am not."

She breathed a sigh of relief and curled up against him. "I do not want you to look for the leech colony. If you die, I will die too. Promise me you will not go looking for it."

He didn't reply and she stiffened against him. "Promise me, Andric."

"I promise."

DANI PAUSED IN THE DOORWAY OF THE COMMON ROOM AND stared at her father. He was sitting in an armchair next to the fireplace, staring moodily into the flames.

"Hello, Dad."

He glanced up and smiled at her. "Hello, my love. How are you feeling this morning? Did you sleep okay? Do you -"

He inhaled deeply, and Dani's heart broke a little at the look of sorrow that briefly flitted across his face. "Andric returned to you."

"Aye, he did." She crossed the room and sat down on the floor beside the chair. She rested her head on his leg and he stroked her blonde hair.

"I imagine he was surprised to see you alive, was he not?"

She took a deep breath. "Aye. He's going to stay with us for a while longer, Dad."

Marshall sighed but didn't reply and she looked up at him. "I cannot stay your little girl forever."

He smiled. "Aye, I know."

He smoothed her hair back from her face and she took his hand and kissed the palm of it gently. "I love you, Dad."

"I love you too, Dani." He leaned down and kissed her on the forehead. "Do you love him?"

"Aye, I do."

"Does he love you?"

"I believe he does."

A frown crossed his face. "Believe? Has he not told you that he -"

She shook her head. "Stop, Dad. It does not matter to me whether he says it or not. I love him and want to be with him, and his actions tell me that he loves me too."

"Are you certain, Dani?" he asked worriedly.

"Aye, I am." She stared down at her lap. "I believed that I was in love with Kaden, but now I realize it was only a silly crush. How I feel about Andric is much deeper and stronger than how I felt about Kaden. Does that make sense?"

He sighed again. "Aye, sweet one. It does."

"After the wedding, I want Andric to come back to our home with us. Will you allow him to do so?"

He blinked in surprise at her. "Of course, I will, Danielle."

The knot of tension in her stomach disappeared and she smiled gratefully at him. "Thank you, Dad."

Marshall took her hands and squeezed them tightly. "If you love him, if this is the Lycan you want as your mate, then I will do everything in my power to make that happen."

She blinked back the tears. "Thank you, Daddy. I love you."

"I love you too." He squeezed her hands again. "And you will always be my little girl."

"Hello, Danielle."

Dani smiled as she looked out her bedroom window. "Hello, Andric."

He shut the door behind him and crossed the room to her. He wrapped his arms around her, and she leaned back against the solid warmth of his chest as he placed a gentle kiss on her throat.

She squeezed his clasped hands as he kissed her throat again. "Are you sore?"

She shook her head. "No. I told you – Aunt Avery healed me completely."

He rubbed her lower belly and a slow beat of desire started in her body. "I do not mean that."

"Oh." She coloured a little. "I was a little sore this morning, but a hot bath took away most of the ache."

"Most?" He kissed the line of her jaw. "Perhaps it would help if I kissed it better."

She twitched against him as he slipped his hand inside her pants and cupped her gently. "I – I'd like that, Andric."

"As would I, sweet Danielle."

He moved his other hand to her breast and squeezed it lightly, rubbing his thumb over her hardened nipple before reaching for the buttons on her blouse. "You're so beautiful."

"Thank you," she said. She moaned when he slipped his hand inside her shirt and cupped her bare breast. "But it will be dinner soon."

"Aye. Perhaps we should wait until tonight. I do not want the first time I taste your sweetness to be a hurried affair."

"I guess."

He grinned at her disappointed tone. "I promise I -"

He stopped when Dani stiffened against him. "What's wrong?"

"They're back," she whispered.

He followed her gaze out the window. Leta, her body nearly vibrating with excitement, was throwing herself at Tristan who was striding out from the woods. He caught her and tossed her into the air before kissing her cheek.

They watched in silence for a moment as the rest of the family spilled out of the house. When Sophia and Kaden stepped out from the trees, Andric's hand tightened against her breast for a moment before he released her.

She hurriedly buttoned her blouse before turning to face him. He smiled faintly. "You should go and see your pack."

She stepped forward and cupped his face before kissing his mouth. "Aye, I will. I want you to come with me."

"Danielle, I -"

She kissed him again and then took a deep breath. "It is you I love, Andric. Not Kaden."

A combination of relief and happiness crossed his features and he pulled her tightly against him. "Truly?"

"Aye. I love you."

"I love you too, Danielle."

He kissed her hard on the mouth and she pressed her body against his before grinning impudently at him. "Of course, you do. It was obvious weeks ago."

He laughed and then slapped her lightly on the ass. "Cheekiness like that will get you a spanking, Danielle."

Her grin widened. "Do you promise?"

He laughed again. "Aye, I promise."

"Good." She took his hand and led him towards the door. "Come, let us welcome home our pack."

END

Read Nicholas' story in "Pale Moon",
Book Five in the Red Moon Series.

ABOUT THE AUTHOR

Elizabeth Kelly was born and raised in Ontario, Canada. She moved west as a teenager and now lives in Alberta with her husband and a menagerie of pets. She firmly believes that a person can survive solely on sushi and coffee, and only her husband's mad cooking skills prevents her from proving that theory.

For more information about Elizabeth, check out her website at

www.elizabethkelly.ca

f facebook.com/EKellyBooks

🐦 twitter.com/ElizabethKBooks

📷 instagram.com/elizabethkelly_author

ⓐ amazon.com/Elizabeth-Kelly/e/B00EOHZ0MS

BB bookbub.com/authors/elizabeth-kelly

ALSO BY ELIZABETH KELLY

Tempted Series

Tempted

Twice Tempted

Forever Tempted

Breathless

Tempted Trilogy (Books 1-3)

Red Moon Series

Red Moon

Red Moon Rising

Dark Moon

Alpha Moon

Pale Moon

Red Moon Bundle Books 1 – 3

Red Moon Bundle Books 4 – 5

The Recruit Series

The Recruit (Book One)

The Recruit (Book Two)

The Recruit (Book Three)

The Recruit (Book Four)

The Recruit (Book Five)

The Recruit Series Bundle Books 1-3

The Recruit Series Bundle Books 4-6

The Shifters Series

Willow and the Wolf (Book One)

Ava and the Bear (Book Two)

Katarina and the Bird (Book Three)

Porter's Mate (Book Four)

Bria and the Tiger (Book Five)

Rosalie Undone (Book Six)

The Dragon's Mate (Book Seven)

Rise of the Jaguar (Book Eight)

The Draax Series

Reign (Book One)

Rule (Book Two)

Rebel (Book Three)

Harmony Falls Series

Sweet Harmony (Book One)

Perfect Harmony (Book Two)

Forbidden Harmony (Book Three)

Redeeming Harmony (Book Four)

Individual Books

The Necessary Engagement

Amelia's Touch

The Rancher's Daughter

Healing Gabriel

The Contract

A Home for Lily

Saving Charlotte

Shameless

The Fairy Tales Collection

Broken

An Unlikely Seduction

Holiday Romance

The Christmas Wife

The Christmas Rescue

The Christmas Nanny

Sordid Games